JASMINE THE LAST PHOENIX

JASMINE THE LAST PHOENIX

Book 1

By
Lisa Colt Jarvis

© 2022 Lisa Colt Jarvis

All rights reserved. This book or any portion thereof may not be reproduced or used in any manner whatsoever without the express written permission of the publisher except for the use of brief quotations in a book review.

ISBN: 9798356695766

CHAPTER 1

JASMINE

This time of the morning is the absolute best. Everything seems possible. I don't quite know if I am awake or asleep. The calm before the storm. I hear my father's footsteps walking across the floor above me—the slight creaking of the floorboards, the weird rubbing sound as each foot makes contact with the floor. Why do I feel so safe and cozy just because of a sound? My thoughts drift as I start to fall back to sleep as the coffee machine makes the distinct sputtering noises. What was I just thinking? Oh, the smell of coffee. Dad moving through his morning like a dance. Ha. Maybe I am still sleeping.

"Tiffy." I hear his deep voice try to keep a whisper as he calls down the stairs to my dog. I could do without this morning habit. I know he is waiting and listening to the point of holding his breath, hoping to hear the jingle of the dog, Tiffy's collar. I listen but hear nothing but the spit and gurgle of the coffee machine. "Tiffy!" This whisper is accompanied by a light slap on his thigh. Again, I hear nothing, just Dad making his breathing shallow to hear better. I know he is getting frustrated with the dog, and the smell of his waiting coffee is getting the better of him. I hear the toaster click, hear the shuffle of his feet, then he is at the top of the stairs again. He returns to the business of calling the dog so he can let her out. "Tiffy!" His tone is firm, but he still tries to keep the hush. He claps his hands together. He takes a deep breath and lets it out with force. "Tiffy!" The whisper and any hush are gone. His irritation is making him forget he is even trying to be quiet.

I slowly open my eyes and look at the reason for Dad's anger. Little black eyes are already looking back at me. I have to smile at this little face, my beautiful dog with her black curls and strange eyes. Sometimes round and brown like other dogs and sometimes green and shaped like reptile eyes—I love this dog. I don't know why she's so different from other dogs, but she's always been here. Her fur never grows very long, and her temperament's always good. Except when she won't listen to Dad. I've had this dog for as long as I can remember. I've never been without Tiffy. As I watch Tiffy close her eyes, I close mine also. I pull the covers over my head, but I know I'm going to be getting up soon. Oh, if I could just go back to sleep. What was I dreaming again? It was a good dream about flying. I was a great bird, a great bird that breathed fire. I squeeze my eyes shut, trying to get back to the place in my dreams, my light dreams, my awake-in-my-sleep dreams.

"Goddamn it, Tiffy!" The voice is now thundering. I take a deep sigh, and Tiffy follows with a sigh of her own. Tiffy kicks her little dog legs a few times but shows no sign of getting up and is not even opening her eyes. I turn my head to check the time on the alarm clock. It reads 7:14—nowhere near any normal summertime wake up, but somehow this is about the time I have gotten up all summer. Most teenagers my age get to sleep all day. Oh, well. I grin and turn my head back to the dog who still has her eyes closed. I follow my dog's lead. Nose to nose, we hope the angry man will stop soon. I laugh to myself. Tiffy must be having a great dream too. The brief moment of hope is dashed away.

"When I call you, you had better come." This time it's not just the voice coming down the stairs. I hear my father, Alfred, smashing each footstep down the stairs. Finally, Tiffy gets up and jumps down from the bed. She has time to stretch her legs out, and as she finishes the back legs, a large, enraged Alfred is filling the door to the bedroom. He is tall and thickly built. Tiffy runs to the far side of the bed. "You better come here, Tiffy." The calm, quiet morning has left this man and the house. He is red in the nose and the cheeks.

I turn to look at Dad, who kind of looks like Santa when he's like this. "Dad, what are you doing?" I smirk, trying to defuse his anger and save Tiffy. It is a silly way to wake up every day. I have never understood why Dad does the same thing every day or why Tiffy won't just go out and pee. Both father and dog are silly.

"Well, Darling, I wanted to let Tiffy out so you could sleep in." His tone is quickly tender and slightly apologetic.

I lift my body part way up and use my arms to slide myself up into a sitting position. My long curly tangles are stuck to my face and under my behind as I grin up at my father. It takes a moment for me to get untangled. "Dad! I'm up now." I raise my eyebrows and shake my head in a "yes" gesture. It doesn't make sense to be this loud and demanding just to keep the house quiet. I try to hold back my laughter at this logic. For two years these two have done the same dance. Dad trying to get Tiffy to pee and Tiffy not moving. It always ends the same. Dad and I having the same conversation. I would not have it any other way. I am laughing hysterically as Tiffy jumps back up on the bed and lies down behind me in the warm spot I left from my body, safe from Alfred. With a loud snort, she turns in a tight circle and goes back to sleep. I scratch my messy tangled hair, wrinkle my nose, and laugh. I can see the last bits of Dad's anger dissipate. He looks at me.

"Sorry, my darling." The red is slowly leaving his face. His wonderful face. I had not noticed how much it has aged. The wrinkles seem to suit him, the slightly receding hair line and thinned out hair. I can see his scalp through the combed-back locks. I love this face. It has aged but is still the same face that is my everything. "Did you sleep well?" He speaks softly.

"Yes, Dad, I did until you started screaming." I lift my brown eyes to look him in his gray eyes. This is our morning routine. I can't understand why he doesn't just leave Tiffy. She never goes upstairs this early. I reach behind me, feeling the soft black body. I grab Tiffy and put her on my lap. I pet her with my long brown fingers. Oh, how I love my childhood companion. There has never been a time when Tiffy was not part of my life.

"Well, why don't you get dressed, and we'll get something to eat," Dad says with a big laugh.

"OK, Pops, but could you please stop trying to *help me* in the morning?" I smile, showing all my teeth to him. My father chuckles at me as he turns to leave. Tiffy jumps off my lap and the bed, follows him up the stairs, runs to the front door, and scratches with her front paws to go out.

"Damn dog! Why don't you listen?" I can hear the fondness in my father's voice as he softly scolds the dog.

Dad and I spend the first part of the day cleaning, getting ready for the start of the school year. We have a weekend to-do list. Today there will be extra because I have to go through my closet. We start with washing the car, cleaning up the house, washing the dog, and doing the laundry. I see my dad's face change as he kisses my forehead and moves upstairs to his room. I think about his face for a moment. His smile dropped to almost tears. Why did he look so sad? Did I just imagine it? I turn to follow him up the stairs when my phone rings. Gosh, I have waited all morning for her to call.

"Hannah." I answer my cell phone and turn away from my father's path.

"She is making me try *on* the clothes. I hate this, and I hate her!" an angry voice snaps at me. I break out laughing so hard that I pee just a little. I run down the stairs to change.

"Hannah, you just made me pee my pants!" She is my soul mate, best friend, sister, and more.

"Jasmine, you said, 'Be nice to Susan. Susan cares about us and loves us.' You said she wants what is best for me." Hannah is running out of air as she speaks but does not stop to breathe in. I try to cover the end of my phone so she can't hear in case I laugh. "She doesn't. I don't want the clothes she is picking out." I hear Hannah take a long, deep breath, replenishing her air loudly.

"Putting you on speaker," I yell as I put the phone down and change my bottom half. Why do we all say that? I wonder, "putting phone on speaker" when no one else is around. "Are you home yet? I like the stuff you sent pictures of. I think Susan has good taste." I just don't understand Hannah's hatred for Susan. She is nice and knows what we like. I think she is so cool. But Hannah is my best friend, so I can't let Susan know I like her too much, at least not in front of Hannah. "You look good in anything, Hannah." I am not exaggerating. Hannah is tall, has naturally blond hair, and looks like she has spent her life in an expensive salon. Hannah has flawless, pale skin, never a blemish. Well, I have never had one either, but Hannah is so tall and perfectly proportioned.

"I have to go. The vampire is coming. See you later, Jasmine. Love you," she says, ignoring the compliment, as always.

"Hannah, you have to help me with my room. Love you too. Be nice to Susan." Why did we start calling her a vampire? So weird and random. I look around my domain, scooping Tiffy up in my arms as I walk from room to room. My bedroom is huge. I have a small den, and my TV is here, then the guest room, bathroom, and laundry room. There is not much for me to do, just my clothes in the closet. I set to work, going through my closet and cleaning my room. I have made a delightful place on the bed for Tiffy to watch me. I place a doggy hat on her and get to work.

CHAPTER 2

SUSAN

"Wasn't that a wonderful time?" I casually exclaim. "It's nice that we are closer in age than most. I know what's in, and I can wear today's fashion." I talk more to myself in the mirror than to Hannah. I know Hannah is not listening. It doesn't faze me at all. I am many years older than I look. Not to toot my own horn, but I frickin' look amazing. Worry is not going to affect my skin. Besides, I have seen much worse than a child who is struggling from being abandoned by her parents. It is my job to look out for her. It is my job to look out for all the kids who were placed here. I walk over to Hannah and caringly brush the hair that is falling into her face with my fingers. Hannah snaps her head away and simultaneously swats my hand. I can feel Hannah's irritation.

Hannah has no idea why I, her dad's girlfriend, am always touching and talking to her like I care. I am working hard to be part of what Hannah is doing. It's exhausting for Hannah to deal with me. She doesn't want to get close to anyone. I get it, but it is my job to keep them hidden and safe from the others looking for them. I have been stuck dating the world's most selfish man, just to get myself close to them—Hannah's father and all his many girlfriends around the world. I know of the girls, and I do not care. It's less work for me than if he were underfoot. This way I can just focus on the kids. I can't stand him, but it puts me safely in the middle of the kids, so here I stay. I may end up breaking my vow not to kill humans, just for this man. I picked Hannah because she is the easiest to mind read, well, the most pleasant. Most are boys, so there is too much sex on the mind. Jasmine is covered, and the other no one talks to as much.

"I don't care about fashion the way you do. Thanks for taking me. I must get a run in before I go to Jazzy's." Hannah has had enough of me for today.

"You are going to Jasmine's? Send her our love. I know you have had enough of me, but I don't know why. I am frickin' awesome." I'm laughing to myself at my own joke. "Oh, that's right, it's Sunday. What a nice tradition you all have. We should start something here!" Man, I wish I could get the kids together and enjoy them the way Alfred does. I could start training them. "Did you eat? Please eat before you run. You are looking so slim." The last comment didn't sound like a compliment. I know that Hannah doesn't eat on purpose, and when she does, she uses drastic measures to correct the calorie intake. Hannah needs to be strong. Hannah also has to learn how to deal with life. I am not here to fix life for these kids. They have to learn and become more resilient.

"We can't do anything here; it is not the same. I eat there with them, my family. Alfred will drop me home in the morning," Hannah says as she grabs her bags.

I bring the few groceries to the kitchen. I listen to Hannah through her mind. Not to be nosy but to know where Hannah is. I put the groceries away and grab my special drink from the wine fridge. I go to my room to drink alone, keeping my mind on Hannah. Not that Hannah would ever come to me, but just in case. Hannah and her father think these special drinks are medicine for a rare blood disease. Well, it is kind of true. I smile to myself, feeling better from the unique nutrition.

Hannah brings her bags to her room. I lie back and listen to Hannah's thoughts in my slightly euphoric state, having just eaten.

Hannah got a bunch of stuff she is never going to wear. It's just to get shopping over with. Hannah laughs to herself because Jazzy texted her about every hour, reminding her to be nice. Jasmine is such a nice girl. She sends Hannah pictures of clothing she wasn't sure if she should keep or get rid of. Hannah would have taken Jasmine's clothes, except Jasmine is shorter. I like trying to build a relationship with Hannah. Haven't had a challenge in a while. Still smiling to herself, Hannah fixes her ponytail, changes into a T-shirt and shorts, and takes off on her daily run. It is the best thing to help clear her head. She cannot describe the feeling but needs it. Leaving her bags on the bed unopened, Hannah goes for a run.

I get up feeling better after the nourishment, and I go down to Hannah's room to put the new clothes away. It is what I like to do. Days here are so boring. But one of my gifts is my ability to withstand the sun and read minds, and that put me at the head of the list for being their protector. Still, I am homesick for the life I had, we all had. I can't wait to go back home. Soon. The time is finally coming.

To my little island, where there are no cars. We still use horses. Well, I laugh, we don't use horses. The humans do in the daytime. During the day, every human does their job. There are not that many. Lots of young and very old. There is a small pack that we have put all our hopes on. I miss watching them train. I was in charge of their minds—meditation and controlling their whisper and shadow. A human's whisper is like the make-believe friend kids have or the guardian angel. It is a part of you and a part of heaven. It is your conscious. A human's shadow is part of you and connects you to the earth and your desires or needs. If you keep them in balance, life works well; out of balance, you are considered selfish or simple minded.

My kind has many whispers and shadows. But we only connect to the earth. We are banned from the heavens, all but my sister.

How I miss watching three-year-olds learning the art of fighting, ten-year-olds running with wolves, and the young twenty-somethings now able to do battle. Oh, and the parties, the other creatures and spirits of the island, the underground city, the shops, and the clubs. My people drinking my drink with others like myself. It is not much longer now. I will bring the children home soon, to where they belong. My island, their island.

CHAPTER 3

JASMINE

I hear the front door upstairs open with a burst of laughing and loud voices. Tiffy jumps from my bed and beats me upstairs. Her little tail is wagging so hard that her whole hind end moves. As I come up the stairs, I see her dancing on her back legs. A moment later, I am scooping her up and greeting my people, my friends, my family. Seth is first to grab me and toss me over his shoulder. His strong muscles barely flex, reminding me I need to beef up since I can't get taller. "I don't see anyone. Do the rest of you?" He puts me down and looks over my head. Aaron, Lance, and Grant join in the fun, pointing out my lack of height.

"Leave her be." Hannah comes to my defense as she passes me to be the first to get to my father. "Pops," Hannah squeals in delight at being the first and jumps in his arms to receive her bear hug. The four boys turn their attention from picking on me to greeting my father.

"Pops!"

"Hey, Pops, thanks for coming to tryouts."

"Yeah, thanks, Pops."

They we are all his kids. Our history runs deep. Our mothers were best friends. All seven of them moved to this small town together. They all married local men. We were adopted at the same time. Yes, amazing, I think to myself as I look at my little tribe, as we used to be called by our parents. Hannah, Seth, Lance, Grant, Aaron, and Penny. The same day even! It was the talk of the town for a while. It has kept our friend group extra tight. Almost daily we are together, except for Penny. It may be because of all the rumors, stories of us being witches, vampires, and werewolves. None of us or our parents cared. None but Penny and her family. Five years ago, my mother was found with her throat ripped out. Seth's, Aaron's, and Hannah's mothers all disappeared within a week during that time. Penny is not allowed to be with us at all. It isn't our fault this all happened. I always thought her mother was mean to the rest of the adults. Penny's mother didn't like us very much either. She was always staring at me with a disapproving look. She didn't come to my mother's service and stopped communicating with everyone. I feel sorry for Penny. None of the others do, but it can't be easy for her. She is still part of our tribe as far as I am concerned. Dad is the only one who pays attention to us all—Seth, Lance, Grant, Aaron, and Hannah. He tries to go to all the games and meets. Once Susan came into the picture, she joined in with being there for us. I'd really like it if my dad had someone to help him love us.

Hannah and Grant have dated since elementary school. This is the way Sunday dinners have gone for the last five years since my mother passed away. I love the way it feels to have everybody around me. Hannah and I sit down on large floor pillows, and I put Tiffy on my lap. We laugh and talk as we open our chopsticks and rub them together. Hannah carefully picks out all of the vegetables and puts them to the side of her plate. My dad and the boys are watching football and laughing. They all stand up and scream at the television during exciting parts of the games. Lance gets up and gets my dad a beer whenever it is low. They talk about their football practice and how they think they're going to do this year. Grant, Lance, Aaron, and Seth have been on the football team since middle school. Lance is a captain. Aaron is a cocaptain.

Lance's phone rings. The room gets quiet. We all know what it means. Lance's mom.

"Bonny?" Dad asks when Lance hangs up the phone.

Lance takes a deep breath. He shakes his head up and down. "Yeah," he says in a controlled voice. "I got to go."

"Take care, son. Let me know if you need anything." Dad's voice is low and emotional.

"Are you all right?" I step up to Lance. I know it is a stupid question, but I can't think of what to say. I look up at him with my eyes wide, trying not to show how upset

I feel. Hannah moves to Grant and slides her hands around him, putting her head against him. He wraps his arms around her.

"Of course, silly. I'll text you later." Lance smiles at me and pats me on top of the head.

"I gotcha," Grant says as he kisses Hannah on top of the head and lifts his arm from behind her back, over her head. I scoop up Tiffy and go to my father. Hannah goes to the other side of Dad. Lance looks over at us and smiles at us. All the boys leave to get Bonny from whatever trouble she is in. After the boys leave, we finish picking up. We text and speculate about what has happened. Dad lets Tiffy out. When he lets her back in, he locks the door, kisses both us girls on the forehead, and goes up to his bed. I hear him cry. His heart breaks for Lance, but there isn't much we can do.

CHAPTER 4

SUNG-GI

I open my eyes from my restless sleep. This is the most important day of my life. It's the most important day of the life of the village, my village. Smiling to myself, I listen to the gentle snore of my sister and the quiet beyond that. Everyone in the village, my village, spends as much time without the sun as they do with. I can see in the moonlit night as well as if it were day. We have been trained to. The vampires who provide for us are night people. Today the villagers in my world, our little island, get to sleep in. Gosh, I have a lot to do today and want a little time to myself. I try to slide my body out of bed, but I have to first lift my sister's arm that is flung over my waist. I try carefully to move my sister, Shinan-Hua, only to have her wrap her leg around and squeeze me even closer, murmuring something I can't understand. I finally untangle from her and get out of the bed. I turn and flash her an irritated look that falls upon a dead-asleep body. Smiling to myself, I pull up the blanket that my twin sister has kicked off and cover Shinan-Hua back up. I look down at my sister, who slightly twitches as the blanket touches her.

For twenty-two years, we have shared a bed. Last night, this moment, is the last time we will be in the same bedroom. I grab a wooden bucket. I look at myself in the mirror. My heavy bangs kiss my eyelashes. I look up slightly, crossing my eyes, and see the black tips as they tickle my lashes. I grab a pair of scissors and cut a tiny bit off them. I have a slight bend to my hair. My amazing twin sister has a real wave. Shinan-Hua has the most beautiful hair, the best of our small tribe, but my crazy warrior sister cares nothing for things like taking care of her hair. It is always up in two braids with a part in the center. I unbraid my own hair, letting a wavy-patterned mess fall free. I study my reflection. My eyes are mahogany brown and almond shaped. They look back at me excitedly. My nose ever so slightly scoops up. My sister's is straight. The difference is so slight that most can't notice. My sand-colored skin almost glitters like Alexandra the Amazonian vampire. I stick my tongue out at myself and crinkle up my nose. Turning, I grab a scrub brush, soap, and towel, putting them in the bucket, and I throw clean clothes over my shoulder. I look in on Shinan-Hua before I head out the door. All the houses have plumbing. The vampires who look out for the villagers have made sure the village is as modern as they can, although there are no televisions or phones.

There is only one villager who has a line of communication outside of their little world. Even with their fancy bathrooms, most of the villagers clean up at the river that flows out to the ocean. This is where I am heading on my own.

A little outside the village, I slow down to do my morning meditation. I put my wash things down. Breathing in, I slowly sink into an almost-seated position. As I lift my arms up, my thoughts melt away. I become one with everything. My mind stops, and something else takes over. My whisper and shadow are as excited as I am. They inform me that most of the village—up and down the city, the water people, the creatures of the earth and sky, the spirits, and pretty much everything on this island—is looking forward to today. My arms drift to the right of my body. The slight current of air moves with me as the energy around me gently moves. My inner conversation continues. I smell the flowers and trees. The conversation becomes just knowing and feeling. I hear the wind moving leaves. My breathing, my body, and the world around me dance with my movement.

After some time, my mind settles back with my whisper and shadow in balance. I take in my last breath and stand as I exhale. I walk to the river and wash up. The cool water is refreshing against my skin. The water swallows me up to my neck. I swim for a bit, enjoying the quiet sound of the water pushing and pulling against itself because of my disturbing it. I grab a crude piece of soap. It has a special smell to it. I use this soap only for special times. This piece I have had for a long time, and I brought a full, fresh bar of my special soap. Julie, who leaves the village for half the year, brings it back with her every spring. I have a full box of it, but I think it is so special that I can't allow myself to use the perfumed soap every day. Julie tells us that special soap like this is used daily. When we bring this village back to its former glory, we will have special perfumed soap we all can use every day. Today I am happy to use it. I wash thoroughly, enjoying the smell and the bubbles as they drift out with the current.

Married, today—I am going to become Ryo's partner. I am going to have babies. Together we are going to bring this village back to its former glory. Ryo and I have been talking and planning just how we are going to do this. It is all so much; I think I am ready for this challenge and the important role. I am going to become a woman. Mostly all the villagers are my age and younger. This is going to be the first physical relationship in this generation. I finish washing up, blushing at the thought of what is to come with Ryo later. I brush my hair as I hum to myself. Pulling my bangs out, I put the rest of my hair up in to three connecting ponytails down the center back of my head. I place everything back in the bucket except my towel and night clothing. I use my special soap and clean my night clothes. I breathe in the smell as I wash everything. I hang it all up on a tree limb. I would come back for them, but most of the time they show up back at the house. I will have a new house.

I wonder if whoever or whatever brings me my clothes will know where to bring them? Most likely. The whole island is going to be at our wedding. First time I know of that all the creatures will be together. Things can go very wrong when all the creatures are together. It will be OK. Precautions have been taken.

My mind comes back to the present. I love the quiet of the morning. I can feel the eyes of the wood creatures who are always around but barely ever seen. I am smiling to myself because you are never alone here. A brief feeling of sadness crosses my mind as I think of my parents and the younger sister I lost years ago, wishing they could be with me now. The moment passes. I live my life for them. For the memories of them. To someday avenge them. Not today. Today is just for me and those who have survived. Most mornings all the women of the village would be here with me. But today is special for the whole village, mostly for Ryo and me. I sing to myself as I walk up from the river after washing. This really is going to be a day that makes history.

I feel the shaking of the earth and hear the breaking of branches and ground debris rustle. As I lift my head, I see a pack of over fifty wolves. The musty smell of fur fills the air. The panting of so many large beasts makes the air humid and adds to the smell—death. They must have been hunting. They are going to eat today. Why hunt? They probably have energy to burn or want to be ready in case anything goes wrong. The oversized wolves pick up their speed and trot into a semicircle around me. A large but thin wolf breaks from the others and comes slowly toward me. The others sing out in soul-piercing howls.

"The wolves are back!" A small voice cries out in joy.

Ten little fairies run toward the wolves from the far side of me. I hadn't even sensed them, not that I ever do. The wolves turn as one, except the female approaching me. She transforms into a tall, slender human and continues forward. She bows before me and gives me a warm hug. I hug her back. My guardian and friend for life and beyond. Shino, my strong, beautiful wolf. When we are born or brought here to this island, we are matched with a wolf until death.

"Congratulations."

This is her only word before she transforms back into a wolf and takes her place beside me, brushing her heavy, furry body against me lovingly. The soft fur slightly tickles my waist. By now the ten fairies are jumping higher and running faster than the werewolves.

There is nothing like a fairy. Each in its natural state stands about three feet high. They look like small human children but have unlimited strength, the ability to fly, extraordinary speed, and jumping power. They are the ultimate being. They have all the magic of any other being. They can transform into anything—creature or plant. With thousands of different creatures that humans outside of the island no longer believe in but we harbor, we grew up learning of their stories and what they look like from the fairies changing into each one of them. These small, powerful creatures are everything to me and my village. Their love and free spirit make one want to protect them, even though they are the very alpha and omega of earth. They are whispers and shadows, totally connected to heaven and earth. They have no enemy that can win against them head on, but they can be easily tricked. Their nature is to protect the earth. All the plants and living creatures are protected from evil when the fairies are able. Of the almost one hundred fairies on the island, only one is male. He no longer comes to the human village, not since the destruction sixteen years ago, when he was tricked into fathering my sister and six other babies for the evil group of vampires. When the babies were born, the vampires killed our village to get them.

"Ryo and Sung-Gi's day!" A very deep-brown skinned fairy interrupts my thoughts. Her beautiful large eyes twinkle as she looks over at me before grabbing a wolf and hugging him.

"Yes, special day, today!" another says as she jumps from the back of one wolf to another.

"Beautiful Ryo and Sung-Gi!"

"Let's go get ready for the day," the beings say as they tumble and roughhouse with the wolves. They make their comments sound like songs. The playfulness and laughter are infectious, filling the wolves with so much joy that they are like puppies. Fairies can move faster than the eyes can follow. Every once in a while, I lose track of one just to see her in a whole different area.

The fairies are so joyful. They are making the flowers around them burst into full bloom with just a touch of their hands, jumping on and around the huge hairy animals, causing a beautiful chaos.

I try to sound authoritative and strict to keep them focused. Still, I cannot help but smile as the moon illuminates the scene of werewolves and fairies. I can still feel the eyes of the others on me as I give one of the fairies my clump of soap.

"It's a special day for you!" The large brown eyes stare up at me as the small brown body of the sweet creature comes to a stop in front of me. The fairy smiles up at me.

The rest of the fairies each have their own distinct complexion and hair combination: red hair, black hair, blond hair, and any combination in between. None are the same, and they come over to me, giving me hugs, kisses, and hugs again. I smile as I hug them back, knowing this will be going on for a while. I am grinning from ear to ear, and each hug the fairies give is so sincere with love, gratitude, heart, and repetitive. I had taught them when I was young to stand in line. They line up again after hugging and kissing me.

Finally, I say, "Yes, my little lovelies, could you help me by washing these wolves until they smell like mint, lavender, and jasmine?" I widen my eyes and raise my eyebrows.

A little red-haired fairy shakes her head. The red loose curls move with such force in agreement. Her green eyes, large and round, are mimicking me.

The fairies have found something else to hold their interest, but the wolves heard what was going to happen to them; a howl broke out, followed by a few wolves being tossed in the river by happy, giggly fairies. The wolves that have landed in the water look miserable as they swim back to the water's edge. Fairies love to have fun and are part of the natural world. They can alter nature and have no predators, so they have no fear. They are kind and loving beings with truly not a care in the world on one hand but all the weight of the world on the other hand. They try to keep the natural balance, but humankind has upset it so much that this little place, this island, is what they control for now.

"Shino will wash later." I signal to the wolf next to me. I push my hand through her fur. "Sekiya may need to check with Ryo, so she should hurry," I say, speaking about my soon-to-be husband's wolf. I stand a bit taller at the sound of that.

I watch as the group makes its way to the water. The fairies are interested again, and they see a chance to play.

"Human form also. Pull all the ticks from yourselves. Let's get you all clean to the skin," I call out as I walk away, getting an instant replay of sorrowful howls. I laugh as we walk back to the village. My hand rests comfortably on Shino's back. I can feel the heat from Shino's body. It comforts me, like a child is comforted by their mother holding them. When Shino was a puppy, I used to lie on her. I remember her heat and heartbeat. It is what I go to when I need comfort. I just lie on her, and we watch the stars or the sky.

CHAPTER 5

JASMINE

I slide joyfully into one side of the booth in the corner of the restaurant. My hands remain firmly wrapped around my new cell phone. I feel like I haven't stopped talking or smiling since my dad accidentally woke me and Hannah up this morning while he was trying to let Tiffy out. After dropping Hannah off, we took off to get ready for school. It is our annual back-to-school shopping trip. I know Dad likes our time together but doesn't see the difference in clothes. I really have tried my best, once again, to explain. The back of his car looks like we have gone Christmas shopping for a small town, not the start of the school year. We have grabbed a few things for Lance, Seth, and Aaron. The boys have school, football, and work, so for them there is not much extra time or money. Dad always gets clothing for them and anything else they may need. They are on our phone plan. Grant's father helps also. Now so does Susan. I love when we have the boys try on what we pick out for them. It is so weird; they have always been like brothers. Lately, Seth has been giving me stomach bubbles, and I feel shy around him. It is embarrassing.

The last thing Dad did was surprise me with the new cell phone. I can't believe he got the right one. Hannah must have, no, Hannah *would* have told me. One of them had to have helped him. He didn't use Google or any other search engine on the internet, so he didn't do this himself. Who cares? This is the best. As we sit to eat and I work on transferring one phone to the other, I talk about what we got for the boys.

"Do you like the phone?" Dad asks with a smile.

"Uh...yeah! I can't believe you got this for me. Thank you! Thank you! Thank you!" We continue to talk about who is taking what classes this year. I couldn't believe that Dad got a few things for himself too. We both order a bacon cheeseburger and cheesy fries. I get a water, and Dad orders a tall beer. I busy myself with showing him all the features of my new phone.

"Jazzy, I have something I need to talk to you about." Dad takes a big gulp of the beer as soon as the waitress brings it. I stop talking and look at him. I notice his face drop. I cock my head a little after hearing his tone. Dad snorts out a small laugh. "You remind me of Tiffy right now." I grin as I look at my father. I see his expression is becoming serious. Gravely serious. "I have a new job, Jazzy," he starts with a big smile. I don't believe his smile. There is something sad behind it.

Until the words sink in. A job! Pop has wanted to work. This is great.

"Oh, Pops! That's great!" I breathe a sigh of relief. I thought from his tone and face it wasn't going to be good news. This is the best day, and nothing is going to ruin it, I sing to myself. I text Hannah and the others as Dad talks. Hannah and the rest quickly reply with "congratulations." I lift my head up and focus back on my father, relaying the messages from Hannah and the others.

"Let me finish, Darling…listen. Yes, it is great. This is an amazing opportunity for me. I really need to get back out there and work….But…it's far away from here, Jazzy." I freeze.

"We're moving?" Terror grips my whole body.

"I'm not going to move you from here or our house," he calmly reassures me. "What it means is I'm going to travel during the week. I have to leave tonight for three days—orientation and paperwork, things like that."

My mouth is slightly open. I lean forward on the table. My eyes are glued to my father's face as he goes into more detail about the job and his comings and goings. Goings as in going to leave me alone. Dad's eyebrows are raised high, and the edges of his mouth turn up uncontrollably as he talks to me. I know he is working to control his face. I see he can't help but to get excited as he talks. It has been years since he's had a job that he could be proud of and one that would really challenge him. First, Mom got sick, and he had to take care of her. After she died, and her friends, who were his family's world, fell apart, he had to take care of me and the other kids—Seth, Grant, Aaron, Hannah, and Lance. How can I be upset? I am so selfish. But I feel upset anyway. I know he is having a challenging time and spends a lot of money because he is taking care of everyone. Ultimately, he is finally going to get on his own feet. Just in time too, because I heard him say money is running low.

When the waitress comes with the food, I slowly sit back and turn my eyes to my plate of food I no longer want. "Jazzy, I'm going to leave you enough money for whatever you need. Jazzy?" Dad lowers his head to try to look into my eyes. I won't look at him. He always does this. My hurt heart is overwhelmed and making my throat burn. "Talk to me." I see his excitement leave him. I can't help but feel worse. I pick up a French fry and twirl it in my fingers. I swallow hard, silently willing my tears to stay put and not come out. My eyes are stinging for release. "I'm sorry, Baby, but I can't turn this down." Dad's voice is soft and expresses concern. I shake my head "yes" in agreement but don't look up from my plate. A large, painful, hot lump rises, stinging my throat. I focus all my energy on keeping it down. "Jasmine." Oh, gosh, there's more, I think to myself. "Honey? Um, there are a few more things."

"A few more, Dad? A few more things!" My tears are disobeying my wishes and falling down my face. My throat burns as my emotions can no longer be held down. "What,

Dad?" I hiss. "What else besides abandoning your daughter, like Hannah and Lance were abandoned? Oh, wait. They still have a parent at home." I am having a tough time trying not to yell. My harsh whispers are coming out in uneven volumes and pitches. A few people are glancing over. I am used to people looking at us. Being Black and having white parents, now just my father, is cause for people to look, but this is embarrassing. I work to control myself again. The large ball in my throat expands no matter what I do. My chest feels so heavy. "Dad?" I lose the battle, putting the French fry down. I drop my head into my folded arms on the table and just focus on my breathing.

"Am I late?" The strange voice was right above me. I look up to find a very tall woman who is standing over me. "You must be Jasmine." The intruder holds out her hand with a big smile. I flare my nose in disgust, pull my eyebrows together, and look at my dad. My dad is turning all shades of red. He turns his ashamed face and scrutinizes his plate.

"Dad?" I am wondering if this is a prank television show. I can't get my head around what is going on. What is wrong with these people?

"Jasmine, your father may not have gotten around to telling you. I am Ursula. I'm a friend of your father." Ursula lowers her hand to shake with mine. She must be crazy if she thinks I am shaking her hand. Dad raises his empty beer mug to the waitress and slides over to make room. Ursula plops down next to him, still eyeing me. She pulls her hand back.

"Dad?" I say again. Totally ignoring the intruder sitting across from me. Why am I so mean to her? I hate myself but can't smile at her. I can't make her feel welcome.

"Your father and I have been good friends since before you were adopted, Jasmine." Ursula ends her sentence by kissing Dad. Dad is as surprised as I am, I think, from the look on his face. He can't meet my eyes. He lowers his head slightly, and his shoulders drop in defeat.

"Well, Penelope, or whatever your name is, I have never heard of you in all my life, so you couldn't have been that close." All the sadness and despair I feel translates into hot anger toward this woman. I have no intention of speaking her name out loud.

"Ursula. My name is Ursula, not Penelope, Dear." There is an icy undertone in her voice. I hear it, but it just makes me feel better about the way I feel and am acting toward her. I don't care.

Dad is thankful that the waitress comes back with his beer. As the waitress clears my and Dad's meal from the table, Ursula orders a full meal, making it clear that we aren't going anywhere soon. I grab my new phone and ignore my dad and this new person, Ursula. Soon both adults stop attempting to bring me into their conversation. Ursula stops trying to be nice and asking me questions. I know her feelings must be hurt. As Dad and Ursula talk, I text my friends, filling them in on my father's new job away. I get a barrage of questions about who I am going to stay with. How can I be left alone at my age? As I am getting texts coming in with questions, I am unloading about Dad's new girlfriend. I get bombarded with apologies about what I am going through and words of what they think are wisdom from each person. A question comes up about whether Ursula is going to stay with me while Dad is away. Shock at the chance of this breaks my silent treatment.

"*Dad!* She is not staying with *me, right?*"

"No, Darling. But you will have her number if you need anything." Dad seems happy I am at least talking, even if it isn't to join the conversation.

"I can stop by to check on you," Ursula chimes in.

"No!"

"No thank you, Dear." The "no" came out in unison, sounding harsher than it was meant to. I am a bit sorry for the way it sounded. Ursula got quiet, and there was a very awkward hush that came over the table.

CHAPTER 6

ELSABET

On top of a forty-foot building, we stand, four statuesque figures. We are watching and listening to the scene below with amusement. Fairies are so playful, older than we are but never jaded by the world. And a beautiful Sung-Gi going slowly through a series of movements below us. I turn my head to view the rest of my world, a world captured on a small group of islands. My magnificent playground. I command authority, although I am the shortest of the four and also the youngest. I was born, then made in the second Viking age, around 1,000 AC. I will never see my Valhalla; I will live forever. Those who believe in heaven of my kind will never make it. Our whispers are cut off from glory of any kind. So I will make this world and the future world my Valhalla, their heaven. My companions who stand with me were born and then made during the span of the ten to hundred years prior.

I stand in my beauty and glory. Half of my hair is pulled back, temple to temple, in a high, tight ponytail on top of my head. The ponytail blends into the rest of my free-falling, glossy, sandy-blond hair, which ends in a cascade at the curve of my strong lower back. My hazel-green eyes are sharp and alert. They are moving quicker than any other part of my body. My long, lean, unwrinkled hand grasps an old wooden walking stick. The stick is one I have held for 190 years as head of my family. I turn my head back to view Sung-Gi and Shino once again. This is what I have created. Before long the special children will join us, and we will spread the love throughout the world that it has lost.

Beside me stands three much taller creatures. Perival is to my immediate left. He stands tall, lean, and proud. Perival, who has been a member of the family since its beginning, with his jet-black hair, is the heart and art of our world. His dark almond eyes, perfectly smooth skin, and ultimate beauty make it hard not to look at him. He stands taller than me but not as tall as the two on my right side. To my immediate right stands Tybalt. Tybalt is the most beloved vampire. His ease and grace, not to mention his love of all sexes, along with his unbelievable memory, make his understanding of each creature that he comes in contact with a strength and a weakness. Also to my right but standing slightly back behind Tybalt is the exquisite Alexandra. Alexandra is taller than everyone. She is the opposite of Tybalt; she couldn't care less about what you are dealing with. She just expects you to do your duty. She is from the direct line of Amazonian women. Her bronze skin almost glistens in the moonlight. She has very light-brown hair with touches of gold at the hairline. Her hair is pulled back in the same fashion as mine. That is all we have in common. Although we all train, Alexandra has a chiseled form, as if made of rock. Nothing on her body moves without her commanding it to. The four of us look down as the human finishes. Sung-Gi and her wolf start walking up to meet us.

I love this human, as I have loved her mother, as I love her sister, as I have and do love their descendants. Before us vampires divided, I watched everyone in her previous generation who served us. Sung-Gi's mother broke down my defenses and, for the first time in centuries, was my best human friend. There was nothing I wouldn't do to keep her safe. I lost all my people and the humans who were under my protection because of it. I cared too much for her, and it got her killed. As much as I care for Julie, Shinan-Hua, and Sung-Gi, I will never get that close again.

I can hear Hannah talking on the phone. I know what is going on. Alfred talked to me about his plans and new girlfriend. I offered more money for him to maintain everyone's life. He said it is not just about the money. I realize he has taken all the responsibility that was supposed to be split between all the families. Darius and his assholes found Jasmine's mother five years ago and ripped out her throat and most likely did the same to the other women who disappeared. Alfred has the right to live given how much he does for all the kids, so I didn't push too hard. I really don't want another human in the situation, but I understand and will have to just adapt. I follow Hannah's mind as she walks Grant to the door. I find a reason to walk out to where the pair are.

"Are you leaving, Grant? What is going on? Hannah, I heard you on the phone. Is everything OK?" Hannah takes a deep breath, feeling exasperated with me. Grant puts his arms around her. They tell me their version of what I already know. "Do you think Jasmine will be OK?" I'm proud of how concerned I sound. Of course the girl will be fine. Humans deal with indescribable torment every day; most of it they do purposefully to each other. These silly kids don't even know what is coming their way or what a difficult time is. They better get their acts together and get tougher.

After Grant leaves, Hannah turns to me. I try not to laugh as she places one hand on her hip and glares as hard as she can. "Jasmine has come a long way in her life," Hannah starts. "When we were younger, Jasmine would get picked on. We have always been by Jasmine's side. All of us—Lance, Seth, Grant, and Aaron. That's what makes us all so special."

I gently push away the thought of Penny. The thought is dismissed. Hannah and I are both so happy and proud that in the last two years, at last, Jasmine loves herself. She has always been joyful, even when the world was falling apart or against her, but she did not always believe in herself and, at times, blamed herself for others' behavior. We all are always surprised at the joy and kindness Jasmine has for everyone. I guess that is why these kids are so worried. Sweet of them, but Jasmine has something special, and this won't shake her. They all do; each one has a gift. I need to be able to work on them finding their gifts. Having difficulties in life makes one more resilient.

"Jasmine has even made friends with those who have bullied her in the past. She forgives everyone. She is always smiling," Hannah continues, explaining the matter to me as though I am a tiny baby. "Alfred was the one person we all could depend on. Now that is falling apart." Hannah picks up a photo on her vanity. It is of her mom, herself, Jasmine's mom, Jasmine, Bonny, Lance, Grant, Seth, Aaron, Penny, and their mothers. Hannah smiles as she caresses the photo with her long fingers. "How wonderful and perfect life seemed for us all then. Well, Lance didn't have it as great."

Lance has a bow in his hair in the photo. He is the only one not smiling. Bonny dressed Lance up as a girl quite a bit. Bonny always drank, but her drinking became much worse after Jasmine's mother died and the families fell apart. Hannah's mother and Lance's father ran away together and have not been heard from. Occasionally, a postcard with a heart will show up for Hannah. I know she is still waiting for them to come home. Now Penny is allowed to do as she pleases and is given whatever she wants. Seth and Aaron both just live in their houses. Their parents don't care what they do, and they have to work for any money they need. Aaron and Seth are like ghosts in their own house.

Alfred kept Hannah and Lance for days at a time after their families fell apart. Bonny kept drinking more and more. I finally demanded that Hannah live full time at home with us. Hannah still is mad about that and blames me. Hannah felt better living with Alfred, Jasmine, and Lance. I know she felt like they were a family there. I want them to feel the same here. It would be more helpful to us all if they were here. Bonny's drinking got so bad that Lance moved back home to take care of her. But every Sunday they gather together and order Chinese food. Alfred always keeps clean spare clothes for when Lance or the other boys come and stay. The door is always open to them. It is the safe haven for the kids. Hannah lovingly places the photo and memories back.

"It looks like the last safe place for us is changing. We are truly on our own," Hannah says.

CHAPTER 7

JASMINE

I remain moody for the rest of the day. I don't know how to control my feelings and don't like being this way, but I can't stop this pit in my stomach from taking over. Dad tries to talk to me a few more times, but every discussion ends in tears. He asks me what I think about going to Bonny's but quickly says that just won't work. Dad is starting to act frustrated and angry. I have never seen him this way. He must work, and this job is an amazing chance for him. It would be nice if some of the other parents could help him occasionally. If it wasn't all on him, he wouldn't have to leave. I know he loves Penny, Seth, Aaron, Grant, Hannah, and Lance, but they all have flakes for parents. The agreement years ago was that they were in this together. They made a commitment to us kids and to look out for each other's families. He is the only one doing it.

I found out that Ursula consulted with Dad about

what to do and has since the job offer came. She is of the opinion that I won't grow if he keeps making things easy for me and gives me my way. Well, I didn't get my way; that is for sure. I have no idea how some woman who doesn't know us can have an opinion about my family. The fact that he is leaving me, and that Ursula knew before me and gave her thoughts about what my own father should do, is so wrong. I will never forgive her. What does she know about us? Nothing!

The time is here. Dad is leaving me for the first time. I can't believe my father only gave me a few hours to process all this, but nothing can be done now. I watch him carry his bags down. I cannot believe he is just leaving. He explains that he is leaving me cash and a blank signed check in case of an emergency. He gives me a hug, but I cling to him. My sobs are loud, raging against how unfair it all is. I see him cry as he packs his car and leaves.

CHAPTER 8

SUNG-GI

"Sung-Gi and Ryo are some of the best we have ever had, save their parents."

I hear Tybalt comment about me, and it makes me blush. I know I am by far one of his top ten favorite humans of all times. Tybalt has been alive for 2,350 years. He is proud, pushing his chest out and slightly straightening his shoulders as I approach. Perival seems to be as proud as Tybalt. Perival has been working one-on-one with Ryo, my husband to be. Perival smiles. "This is going to be the best marriage in a few hundred years."

Elsabet looks at me and speaks. "Sung-Gi, you and your twin, Shinan-Hua, are the perfect likeness to your mother. Each one of you girls has a trait of her also. Sung-Gi, you are the nurturer and confidante, the reason why I love you so." I am shocked at the kind words, but I keep my face from showing it. It is not right to bring into question a comment from one of the vampires.

Elsabet has never shown us much tenderness. We know she cares, but she never expresses it. Our mother was Elsabet's best human friend. I can see that Elsabet is remembering that day when she lost her best friend and became parent to all of us young humans. It must be hard for them all, especially today when, for the first time in sixteen years, we will have an elder couple. The first time in sixteen years that there is hope for growth and children on our little island. For the first time in sixteen years, that hope can set root. A new dawn that has been in the works for years will finally come to light.

Years ago hope was broken and almost destroyed this peaceful village. This village that is tucked away from the rest of the world. Cloaked by a type of mass hypnosis, this 120-year-old village used to be home to a bustling city that was different from any in the world but as up to date as any. A city above and below ground, a city of humans, vampires, werewolves, dragons, gnomes, nisses, multitailed foxes, shadow people (small black shadows that have the ability to help or cause mischief, not a creature's personal shadow; although, they communicate with one another), the illusive cat people, mermaids of both kinds, tree people, elves, and many others plus the fairies. All are still on the island, but their numbers were decimated sixteen years ago. Millions were killed, and only thousands remain. The other creatures are not comfortable living with more vampires and werewolves than humans. So they live throughout the island and will keep hidden until the human and fairy numbers increase. They are working on building their numbers up as they wait for the humans to increase. When this island was built, it was to increase the number of all so the world could be back in balance with nature and the guardians of the natural world. It was a wonderful world in the beginning. Human villagers stayed up all night training or celebrating with vampires or stayed up all day with werewolves and all the other special creatures. The balance of life was perfect. I remember a little of it. I was six when the war came to our island.

When war was waged against the village, ten fairies saved twenty-eight children and seven newborn babies—the focus of their intrusion. The cost was great. Except for the twenty-eight children and seven infants, a thousand or so of the weaker of the town were killed that day. Millions of humans and werewolves gave their life to fight for the freedom of humankind. Now, us young children are grown. Us orphans are coming of age. We are the finest fighters on the planet, human or vampire. We train night and day to become the best, mentally and physically. We are the future and hope for humanity's goodness. I see a single crimson tear glimmer in the corner of Elsabet's eye. She says, "I look at this beautiful girl, her high cheek bones, her skin like deep bronze, her almond eyes. She is all races. She is no race. She is a new race built from the mixing of so many before her. She carries the hope for all." Elsabet reaches for me as I finally reach the top. The sky is turning a dark blue. It will still be hours before the sun comes up. These vampires can be in the sun, but it takes great energy. They will nap until the ceremony, then come and join in the celebration. There are newer vampires who are not as strong. They have been napping for days to be part of today. I bow slightly, lowering my eyes in respect and obedience as I step up to the group of four vampires. Shino lowers her wolf head in respect also. Vampires and werewolves live together and train and share their lives but are, by nature, uneasy of the other because they know the other can kill them. They are matched predators and natural enemies. Respect and courtesy are especially important between them. All four vampires bow back at Shino in return.

"We will see you after the ceremony, my child," Tybalt says as he kisses me on the forehead, and the four get ready to return to their underground home.

"Be happy." Perival places his right hand on my left shoulder. I can feel the weight of it. I smile. He fondly musses up my loose hair right in the front. These may be the nicest words and the nicest gesture Perival has ever shown me. My eyes sting with emotion. Because of the heartache the vampires had when so many of their friends were killed, most are distant and cold to us. Today, the seeds of hope are planted not only in the humans. Vampires are daring to hope.

"Enjoy today. You are becoming a woman and leader in one day. Your mother would be so proud of you," Alexandra says as she hugs me, lifting me off the ground in an unusual display of affection. I am caught off guard and lose my breath for a second. These displays of affection are overwhelming. Shino whimpers a little nervously. She also doesn't know what to do with these new behaviors. She was with me when our world changed. She lost most of her pack. Shino barely remembers vampires being carefree and fun. I can tell she is not liking this at all.

"I will not hurt your human, Shino." Alexandra puts me down, patting me on the same spot as Perival did. She pats Shino as she passes. Shino lets out a yelp and flinches at the unexpected connection. She is now becoming extremely nervous and is flickering slightly back to human form, then returns to her wolf form. If I was not in so much shock, I might have laughed, but this is too much. All this touching.

"You have much to do today," Elsabet says as she caresses my hair and cheek. With no more words or strange touching, the four turn and disappear.

The much-relieved Shino and I head back down to start the day's chores. The vampires start to descend to their underground town to an early rest. The underground town looks much like a regular old-world town, with cobblestone roads just big enough to walk three across. Two-story row houses line many of the streets. Now most of the homes are empty. There used to be thousands of vampires. The day down here was just as busy as the night. The center of the town now has empty shops that still house relics from every era and night clubs and eateries that were open to human, werewolf, and vampire alike. In the middle of the whole lower town is an amphitheater. It is open to the upper village and is the way in and out, up and down, of the two towns. A special dome with a UV shield can be used for daytime events to prevent light exposure. There is a special tribe of wolves that still protect this arena during the day. The bustling vampire village has dropped down from thousands to a couple hundred, and the upper human village that hosted at least three times that number is down to less than fifty, leaving both human and vampire areas looking abandoned and lonely.

CHAPTER 9

JASMINE

I have finally stopped crying. I keep hearing knocking at the door. Tiffy gets to the door first, barking and dancing on her hind legs. I get up once I realize the person is not going away. Looking out, I smile in joyful surprise. He is just who I need to talk to, and we never have time alone anymore. I unlock and open the door. Tiffy runs outside in the yard, happily barking at the shadows. She looks like she is barking at someone in the shadows.

"What are you doing here? Is everything OK?" I step back, letting my friend in. I am glad and thankful to have my crony. They all have always been there for me. I understand, in moments like this, how lucky I am. I gaze at my lifelong friend with love.

"I was worried about you. You sounded so down and alone," he says as he closes the door.

"I know. Can you believe the day I've had?" I turn

and lead the way to the living room. "Where is everyone?" I ask as I sit on the couch, glancing over his shoulder with slight expectation. My spirit starts to lift for the first time since lunch.

"Just thought you might need a shoulder to cry on and want to do that in private." He sits close to me on the couch and puts his arm around my shoulder. I cuddle into him, full of appreciation.

"Oh, that's sweet of you. You really are the best—"

My words are cut off by a forceful kiss. I push both hands forward in an instant reaction. "What are you doing?" I panic and try to push his arms away to get free. He crushes his lips down on mine and pins me to the couch with his body weight. It is like an unmovable force on me. My mind observes the situation from a place outside my body. He places his hands on my wrists and pins them above my head. I instinctually struggle to get my legs free so I can kick him off, but he is faster and uses his body weight to outmaneuver me. I arch my back, throwing my hips up with all my might. He fumbles and falls off the couch. I clumsily run over him, but he grabs me. I trip forward and fall. He drags me backward as he crawls forward. He gets his feet under him and lifts me to a standing position.

"Wait. Wait. What are you doing? Why are you doing this?" I am unprepared for the force of the fist that slams into my face. He is saying something, but my mind slips into two parts. One part is speeding up and becoming very manic. The other is slow and disengaged from emotions. What was happening? I just can't perceive what is going on. My hands go to my face. Something is dripping and wet. It feels weird. The familiar voice is talking, but I can't comprehend it. I look at my hands and see the blood from my face. This should hurt. Why doesn't this hurt? What is going on? A hand comes down on my wrist with unbelievable force and turns my head to face him. I gape into the eyes of my friend, my brother, the eyes of my attacker. I am unable to grasp the situation. He grabs my shoulder and slams me into the wall, knocking all the wind out of me. The slam brings my brain back together all at once. I am still in disbelief as I am dragged into the living room. He throws me down on the floor and sits on top of me. Confusion clouds my unresponsive face.

"Jasmine! Jasmine!" He slaps me. Finally, I put my hands up to defend my bloody face. "Jasmine, just don't give me any problems. OK?" He slams his face down and kisses me. I start to fight back.

"*Noooo.* Get off me!" He is too strong for me and already prepared. He held my hands over my head with one hand and ripped the bottoms of my PJs off with the other.

The house shakes. It seems it is from outside my mind. I think I see a huge eye in the window. My mind is slipping, I think as I lie there.

After he is finished, he gets up, pulls his jeans back up, and does up his belt. "Clean yourself up. Take a nice shower and use ice on your face. It wasn't as bad as you thought, was it? Let's keep this to ourselves, or others will suffer. You want your dad to be able to work. Well, no, you want him home, but I don't think this would be the thing that would make your daddy very happy. He may not look at you the same. And neither would the rest of the guys… besides, you don't want to worry about your dog's safety, do you? Be a good girl and keep quiet." He bends down and gives me a gentle, tender kiss to the forehead, then goes into the bathroom. I don't move. "Lock the door when I leave and take care of yourself." With that he opens the front door, lets Tiffy in, and leaves.

I stand dumbfounded in the shower. Oblivious of the water or its temperature, I wonder what I have done for this to happen. I feel dirty, alone, guilty, and betrayed by everyone. Maybe this is because I was so mean at lunch. Maybe I deserve this. I slowly scrub every part of myself. It doesn't feel like the soap or water can get me clean. Tears are falling as fast as the water. My crying is soft at times and heavy, gasping for air at others. Deep, indescribable sorrow fills me. I wish my mother were there. The pain and grief of missing my dead mother on top of being raped rip me to my bone. As the warm water turns cold, I stand perfectly still. When I do eventually step out of the shower, my skin is cold to the touch. I half dry my hair. My cell phone rings. I snap back into focus. Fear rises in my chest. I see it's my father and start to cry again. How much I want to have the safety of my father.

"Hi, Daddy." I try to hide the sadness and exhaustion from him.

"Hi, Jazzy." He sounds so normal, I think. With this being the worst day of my life, Dad sounds like everything is fine. "I am at my connecting flight. We should be boarding in the next half hour. Jazzy, I know you got hit with a lot today, but this world is full of that. You are a strong young woman, and I need you to understand that I loved your mother, and I wanted you to be ready. I want to be happy and have someone in my life. She isn't going to take the place of your mother. OK?" Dad sounds emotional. I hate that I was so mean to him before he left.

"Daddy, I am so sorry I acted that way." I sob, and the words don't come out clearly. I'm sorry I didn't protect myself, I think to myself. I cling to my father's voice through the phone.

"I know, Darling. I know. Get some sleep, Jazzy. I'll be home Friday morning. I'll call you tomorrow. I love you." My father sounded soothing, and it calms me a little bit.

"Love you too, Daddy." I need to hang up the phone before I give away the fact that I am not OK. I hang up the phone, pull my heels up to my butt, put my head on my knees, and cry.

After I am all cried out, my sorrow is replaced with something else: determination to withstand anything the world gives me. I start in the kitchen, start by cleaning up the house. I scrub every place he was and has ever been the same way I scrubbed my body. My hands are red and swollen, but I don't stop. I want every one of his cells out of the house. I weep every time I think about having to see him. How am I going to face him? What if he tells everyone? I continually try to push the thought from my mind and scrub harder. I must think about this later. I am going to cover all my bases and protect myself and my friends from him. I feel so ashamed.

I sit on the front step while Tiffy is outside, stumped as to how to protect my father and friends. For starters, I am not letting Tiffy outside alone. I open the garage and clean up the workout equipment. Dad always had a gym set up for us. We all took martial arts when we were younger. I spend some time on the treadmill, practicing what I remembered, and lifting weights. Being physical helps a little. I sit on my bed afterward and stare at my phone. I have missed calls and texts from Hannah and the others. Opening the back of the phone, I pull the battery out. I walk the house again, checking the doors and windows. Sitting on my bed again, I think about everything. It all is surreal, and I feel fully alone. He is right. No one can ever know. They wouldn't believe me, and if they did, they would never look at me the same, if they would look at me at all. I talk to myself as I grab a bag of frozen peas and a bag of frozen corn. I crawl under the covers and place the peas on one side of my face and corn on the other. Tiffy sits on me, licking my nose. Thank goodness I have the ability to heal weirdly fast.

CHAPTER 10

JULIE

As the day comes on and the sun gets higher in the sky, the small village, wolves and humans, gathers to the amphitheater. Eyes of vampires, safely tucked into the dark, glow as they watch from a safe distance. The ten fairies from earlier are exploding flower buds into bloom in the center of the gathering. They totally mesmerize with being able to go crazy with different plants and flowers. The only one of two vampires who has no discomfort in the sun, Mystic, stands in the middle of the amphitheater. Beside her I stand, a thirty-year-old girl with brown skin and wildly curly hair down to my bottom, and so does my wolf, Renton. On the other side of Mystic is Sung-Gi's twin, Shinan-Hua, and Shinan-Hua's wolf, Shik. On the other side of me stands Darton and his wolf, Thorne.

With a howl of the wolves, Shino and Sakiya come down the stairs, leading from the human village. They are side by side in wolf form. The humans join in and start to sing and chant. Music seeps in from the vampires' dwelling, echoing and bouncing through all the tunnels. Ancient instruments mix with modern, all to the same beat. Ryo and Sung-Gi walk down to make the first coupling vows in sixteen years. The feeling of joy seeps into the darkest, coldest corners of the island. Wonderful creatures—gnomes, with their short, thick bodies, and nisses, with their slightly thinner bodies—peer down at the human couple. Then the gnomes climb down to see better. The tiny creatures that pixies are, with delicate wings, can swarm into large groups. Today they are in vast numbers. Foxes with multiple tails run back and forth. Little men, women, and children with large frog-like feet cling to the walls. Elves stay close together, keeping their young in the middle. Their sharp, pointy ears and large eyes take the scene in. The cat people, thinner than werewolves in human form, thinner than a human, quietly watch the couple. I try not to stare at them. The others I have seen and interacted with but not these cat people. None of us have ever seen them. They are fascinating. The underground waterway has a small glass peephole for the mermaids. Hundreds of faces are pushed together. The young men and women who know these creatures but never get to see them often stare in amazement. The vampires and wolves try not to look at them so as not to upset them and scare them off. Optimism for the first time in a long time is shown in everything. Even the younger wolves sensed it. It has now started. Life for this little island starts in this moment. Preparation is done.

Sung-Gi is breathtaking. I'm not used to seeing everyone so dressed up. Everyone looks amazing, but Sung-Gi can't be matched. She is like a movie star. She would not know what that is. Sung-Gi has never seen a movie. I live on this island only half the year, and the other half I live with the enemy. But today nothing else matters but this moment. These vows make Ryo and Sung-Gi the head of the human village. They will be named the elders, even though they are the same age as most and younger than me. Shinan-Hua and Darton are to be next in the vampires' plans for marriage. After the ceremony, the vampires, including Mystic, retreat for the rest of the day. The dome is put on so they can look up. The rest of the fairies from the island come and join the humans and other creatures. Fairies are not fond of vampires. So many fairies around make vampires nervous. That is why they have all retired. They dance and sing with their sister fairies. The elves and the nisses play with everyone.

A fairy is born, not made. They are born of a human and the coupling of vampire and human. There is nothing stronger than a fairy. Nothing. Fairies care about nature and the natural balance. They don't concern themselves with fair or unfair, just or unjust, unless the balance of humanity and the natural world would be greatly affected. Vampires can upset that balance and make a fairy go crazy.

Sixteen years ago, the opposing vampires made hundreds of vampires just for this invasion. There were too many, and they wiped out all the humans, werewolves, and most of the vampires. The only ones left alive were a small number of children and puppies that were left with the fairies.

Ryo and Sung-Gi now stand as head of the human village at such a young age. It seems inconceivable to me. But to a tribe that has been trained by vampires and lived as adults all their lives, the two should transition smoothly. Sung-Gi cares for the fairies and the handful of adults who are still alive but not able to function on their own. Sung-Gi and I, sometimes with the help of six others—you can't count on Shinan-Hua—feed the whole human village. I'm with them only for six months. Us female humans help with gardening, fishing, and gathering water. Us females are just as fierce as the men. Fairies, werewolves, and vampires raised us. We all use an instinct that an animal uses. The humans in this village are ten times more acute than a normal human. Being raised, trained, and loved by eternal beings has its perks. Playing with wolves keeps one on their toes also. Breaking up a werewolf fight can be quite something.

I'm different from the rest of the village. I was brought here when I was fourteen. I was a type of elder until now. I can fight but not to the degree the others can. I'm the human mother for all of them, even though I'm only eight years older, and the only one, until now, who showed tenderness to any of them. I spend six months with them, teaching the ways of the human world. The other six months I spend with the vampires who killed the village. I was raised by real humans in the mansion of killing vampires. My mother was used for food. My entire mother's side as far back as can be counted. We have always served the vampires. When the vampire family broke, my mother's side stayed with Mother and her side. My cousin's mother's side came here with Elsabet. When Mystic spent her six months with the other vampires, Mystic would place me with a real, normal human family. Not now, though. But before, I went to school and would come back and teach the ways of humans to the village. Education otherwise was done by the vampires, with my assistance. Sung-Gi and Shinan-Hua learned more than the others. The three of us share a house. I told them things I saw that I was not supposed to know about human lives that they didn't talk about in class. Sex was the biggest one.

Alexandra and Perival work four to five hours every day in the art of fighting: hand-to-hand, sword, tonfa, knife, bo staff, sai, bow and arrow, and any other weapon. They also teach how to fight alongside your wolf, both in wolf and human form. Elsabet works with us on the many styles of tai chi, qi gong, and yoga. Every and all variations are practiced for two to three hours. Tybalt teaches the languages, math, and history. It is extremely fun to hear firsthand accounts of how to adapt to various places and people. I would explain the human life by telling stories about different events and how things in the outer world work.

Most of our learning is done when the sun starts

to set. These vampires can be out in the daytime; it is just uncomfortable and can't be in direct sun, so they use umbrellas and the shade structures set up for them. When the group first lost their parents, Elsabet and Tybalt would stay up during the day. But now Mystic was the only one who would stay up sometimes. Alexandra gets up about two hours before the sun sets to start her practice with all the humans.

Shinan-Hua is the most serious and dedicated of us females when it comes to training. Alexandra has worked separately with Shinan-Hua and Sung-Gi for an extra hour ever since they were little on a fighting style they use together. Shinan-Hua has recently been training on her own also. She is a force when it comes to fighting, but she refuses to prepare for, or clean up after, anyone or their needs or do any other caretaking type of work. She will also be in charge of this village, but she will not feed the people. She just fights. This causes a lot of arguing between her and Sung-Gi, who feels she should do more to nurture the other humans and creatures who may need it. She is to be the second head family for the village. Darton and Shinan-Hua are the next to take the leadership of the village. No one will get married until she and her twin, who is now married, have their marriage and take their places as heads of the village. Darton is also being patient. He is the one everyone expects Shinan-Hua to marry. His temperament is calm and even, unlike Young Sun who runs hot and cold and who has demanded the right to be with Shinan-Hua.

Shinan-Hua fights well with Young Sun. He trains just as hard as Shinan-Hua. There is also Bancroft whose fighting style is like no other. Even though they have all trained together, Bancroft developed a style so different from theirs. He is like this in everything. He moves the village forward by inventing different things to make the day-to-day easier, given modern technology, and modifying it beyond what is in the modern world. I'm always so impressed. I try to always bring back the latest something in technology when I return in the spring.

Darton, Young Sun, and Bancroft all like Shinan-Hua and know being her mate moves them up to a leadership position. She has been told that Darton is her match. You really can't tell Shinan-Hua what to do, even if you are a vampire. Bancroft is perfectly happy becoming Kate's mate. He is not sure how he got in this situation with Shinan-Hua. Kate is kind and easy-going. Bancroft likes protecting her from herself. He smiles whenever I see them together. He talks to me about the situation. Actually, they all do. But he never backs down, and he would want to be third in line. But if Young Sun changes course and marries Shinan-Hua, Bancroft is not sure of his placement. He has planned all his life and was trained to be a decision maker. When Young Sun stepped up and demanded a chance to be Shinan-Hua's mate, Bancroft demanded the right to be included without thinking. Shinan-Hua wants the time to think about her feelings and will not be told who she is going to marry. She cares for them all and admires distinct aspects of each guy. She wants the strongest who not only is going to be the best match for a mate but who will also be able to stay by her side in battle and in leading the village. Shinan-Hua wants a true match in every way. It is also going a bit to her head, all these boys. She loves Darton but wants him to try harder. He is laid back, and everything comes easy to him, so he doesn't exert himself. She wants to be happy and not just be at home having babies.

I think Sung-Gi and Ryo are the perfect match in every way, and that is what Shinan-Hua wants to make sure she has. The love and respect they have for each other has been clear to anyone near to them since they were little. Sung-Gi is ready to have babies. Babies are important because, now that there are elders once again in place, it's going to take a lot to build the village back up to what it once was. The vampires and I, when I come back, are now going to bring orphans from all around the world. Now that the surviving humans are old enough, the rebuilding of family falls on them. As the village grows, there will be lots of responsibilities.

Shinan-Hua thinks that Darton's wolf and her wolf, Thorne, would be a huge benefit. She imagines these, two of the most powerful male wolves, and Ryo's and Sung-Gi's powerful female wolves being in charge of running the wolves. Young Sun and Bancroft have female wolves. Young Sun's wolf in human form is unbelievably beautiful. Sung-Gi and Shinan-Hua are unrivaled beauties in their own right, but Young Sun's

Vanessa is beyond beautiful. Her features are sharp like a canine, but there is a trace of every human race in her. She looks like she was made directly by God's hands. Vanessa is not only beautiful to look at, but she also has a beautiful soul. Shinan-Hua isn't sure why she feels so small when Young Sun's wolf, Vanessa, is in human form. Sung-Gi gets along so well with her. Raeleen, Young Sun's promised girl, hates Vanessa. Because of that, Vanessa spends most of her time with Shino or Sakiya, Sung-Gi and Ryo's wolves. She feels the most comradery with Young Sun. They are dedicated to practicing fighting more than all the people in the village. Bancroft's wolf, Heather, is kind. She is soft spoken and very obedient. Shinan-Hua and I love Heather in any form. Heather is so easygoing. In this village it is hard to separate wolves from humans. When you think of a human and your thoughts and feelings about them, it's easy to blend their wolves in with the person.

Shinan-Hua and I go out to see Sung-Gi. We talk about being married.

"Why do I have to settle for Darton as my mate?" Shinan-Hua asks. She does not like having to go through her sister for everything. Shinan-Hua wants to be in control of her own choices, and her sister being a leader of the village sucks. Considering Shinan-Hua will be in the same situation once she gets married, I'm glad I am leaving for six months. There is a tension that has not been here before. If I didn't leave here for half the year, if I didn't have love for our enemy, I would be leading this village. If my heart wasn't split in half daily, I could help more. The problem is I love the very person who destroyed my home and killed my family's parents and friends.

The village has the best leader in Sung-Gi. She knows how much depends on her and is selfless in her life. She knows she is expected to live the life that was laid out for her and understands the reasons. Shinan-Hua, on the other hand, is stubborn. We all know she loves Darton. More than that, Darton worships Shinan-Hua and will put up with Shinan-Hua's fit until it is done. The only one who doesn't understand all this is Shinan-Hua. "Stop being a brat. What about Raeleen and Kate? You are engaging their men. Don't you feel bad for being so selfish?"

Sung-Gi is trying to stay calm. I don't know why we are having this conversation. It is never going to change anything.

"As leader it is my responsibility to be with the best match." Shinan-Hua pulls out one of her short knife blades. She rolls her wrist, moving the blade quickly to different positions.

"Put that away! We are talking, not training."

"Shinan-Hua, please just listen to us." I try to defuse the conversation.

"You should be the one out of everyone to understand me." Shinan-Hua looks at me with a hurt expression for a moment. I can't help but feel bad. I lower my eyes. Then she turns to Sung-Gi. "Life is training. See, that is why I must be leading. You don't get it."

"Shut up." Sung-Gi is just over the conversation. Shinan-Hua looks frustrated and upset. Sung-Gi softens her voice. "I have an idea. A competition!" Sung-G speaks slowly. "I haven't worked it out, but I think I have an idea about a competition. I want to talk about it with Ryo first. Then we can talk about it again."

CHAPTER 11

It's midmorning, and Lance is standing in his kitchen, mixing a beer with tomato juice. He hasn't heard a peep from Jasmine since that day. He's trying to figure out how to get over to see her by himself when Seth comes through the door. They lightly punch their fists together in the way of greeting. The two boys talk as Lance puts the drink on the table next to a plate of eggs, bacon, and two Advil.

"Mom!" Lance yells out. "You want something?" He turns his attention to Seth who keeps staring at him. Lance raises his hands and eyebrows in a questioning manner.

"I want you to leave Jasmine alone." Seth opens the refrigerator, looks in, and closes it again. He stands up straight and looks at Lance. Seth loves Lance like a brother, but he has always submitted to Lance's affection for Jasmine. His heart can't comply anymore with his friend's wishes. She needed someone by her side always.

"How many times now have you requested that? Still can't oblige, man, sorry." Lance moves past Seth to clean up.

"You won't date her. You won't let anyone else step up." Seth pulls himself up with his arms to sit on the counter.

"What can I say? She's mine always. Always was, always will be. Besides, she's not ready yet." Lance looks at Seth. Neither one is mad at the other. It's been the same talk for over a year. Since no one has made a move yet, they are both fine talking about it. Everyone just assumed Lance and Jasmine are a couple. Lance likes it that way. Seth knows there is nothing between them and has let it go, but now he is not going to sit on the side anymore. There is no reason for Jasmine not to be his. He has more right than Lance.

"We'll see about that," Seth says. "I am going to let her know how I feel!"

"Yesterday may have changed everything, anyway."

Grant walks in the front door as Bonny walks in from the bedroom. Bonny is stumbling a little bit, holding her head. Grant rushes over and helps her sit down. She glances up at him, nods her head in recognition, and downs the glass of beer and tomato juice. "Another, Granty." She hands him the empty glass without looking up and wipes her mouth with the back of her other hand. "You're such a good boy." Grant grins at the boys and lifts his eyebrows in a mocking jester.

"Mom, Grant just came in. I made you all that."

Lance snatches the glass with a smirk. He makes another. Grant grabs it and passes it to Bonny, laughing at Lance. They are joking around for Bonny's affection when Aaron walks in.

"Have you seen Jasmine?" Aaron asks as he comes through the door. "I stopped by last night, but there were no lights on."

"Last night! I told you to leave her alone," Lance snapped, shaking his head in disgust. "What time was it?"

"Are you stalking her?" Grant looked at him.

"Jazz has never not texted us good night," Aaron spat out. "She has always been there for us. Don't get on me for caring about how she is. Lance and Seth, you have fought about her as long as I can remember, and now when she needs us, you guys don't care." Aaron looks at the three of them with disgust. "She's really having a tough time."

"What's wrong with Jasmine?" Bonny puts her fork down and looks at the boys with apprehension. Lance, Seth, and Grant look at Aaron with exasperation. Aaron changes his facial expression to one of regret. The only thing worse than Bonny drunk was Bonny hungover and trying to help Hannah or Jasmine. Afterward, Bonny spent some time pushing and yelling at the boys to tell her about Alfred working out of town and having a new girlfriend. Bonny is mortified for Jasmine and irritated with the boys for not telling her sooner. Decisively, she stands up and declares she is going to go see Jasmine. The boys fumble around to stop her.

"I don't think you should go, Bonny," Aaron starts, but everyone else whips their head around to shut him up with their eyes. Aaron can be a little straightforward sometimes.

"It's your fault. Can't you ever shut your mouth?" Seth hisses as he moves in front of Bonny.

"Mom, you can't go." Lance steps between Seth and his mom. He gently pushes Bonny back toward her room. "I'll go see her once Han gets here. You go get ready." He passes her the beer concoction on her way to her room.

"OK, Lancey. But I want to talk to her also." She is happily pacified with her drink.

It will be a few days before any of them see Jasmine.

CHAPTER 12

SUSAN

I hear Hannah try again to call Jasmine. She slams the cell phone down on the kitchen table beside her salad, the salad I made and am trying to force Hannah to eat because she just won't eat anything or throws it up. Hannah yells out in frustration.

"You still can't get ahold of Jasmine?" I ask, picking my head up from the magazine I am reading. "Shall we go over?" I know what happened to Jasmine. It happens a lot in this human world. Actually, it happens in the vampire and werewolf world. Dealing with difficult things, as my sister Mystic and I say, seasons the creature. In my hundreds of years, the biggest thing I have learned is that the most interesting and dependable creatures are those who are seasoned. One has to learn to push through, and you become even stronger—pressure presents diamonds.

Hannah seems hopeful as I drive her to Jasmine's. As we pull up out front, we can hear Tiffy barking. I watch Hannah go straight for the spare key spot, but there is no key there. For the first time since they could remember, there is no key. Hannah bangs on the door with her fists. She hears only Tiffy. Defeated, I take her home in silence. Hannah thanks me and goes to get dressed for her daily run.

I watch her pull her hair up into a ponytail. The front edges by her temple fall out. Hannah blows in an upward manner to get the hairs off her face. It doesn't matter how old I am; there is something so special about the way hair moves. It is the only body part that follows the path of least resistance. It flies, it floats, it drifts; all the ways it moves are beautiful. Finding myself alone, I grab one of my special drinks. I must stop waiting so long. I was so hungry that I could hear the beat of Hannah's heartbeat in her neck. Grabbing my book, I relax with my blood drink and start reading where I left off. As I get more comfortable, Mystic comes to me. "The wedding has happened. The kids can come back." She tells me all about the celebration. I tell her about the attack on Jasmine and everything that has been going on. We agree it is not something we should concern ourselves with at this point in time. We decided I would keep an eye on the young man to see if he was safe to bring back home or if he is too far gone with desire for power. Mystic filled me in about my family, showing me a mental movie of my home. I can't wait.

CHAPTER 13

JASMINE

"Jasmine," Dad calls out. He came home a few days ago and is leaving today. I am happy to have him home. I just couldn't spend much time talking to him. I didn't know how to talk to him and didn't want him to find out what happened. Dad seems uncomfortable too. I couldn't hide the fact that I am so sad when he got home. He kept himself busy, and we have not done the one-on-one things we thought we would do. He keeps looking at my face; it looks puffy and bruised. He tears up every time he looks at me. He must know I cried a lot to make my face look like this.

Ursula was here for most of the weekend. I apologized to her, but that is about all I said. I was thankful to have her here. Ursula kept Dad's focus off me. Dad got several peeved phone calls from Bonny when her son couldn't get ahold of me. I explain to Dad that I was trying to get used to all the changes. I reluctantly agreed to Sunday dinner with them, even though Dad isn't going to be there. Ursula thought it would be best for the rest of the kids to not be around during that weekend. She said, "It is the first weekend Alfred is home since his new job." I was fine with that. Between me and Ursula, there was a reason for Hannah, Lance, Seth, Grant, and Aaron not to visit. The truth is I've been avoiding the whole crew. I have ignored all calls from my friends. I needed time to think alone. I realize I have never been alone before. I spend the time looking up articles on rape, reading stories, and planning my defense. I am going to conceal the whole event. It is the only way to protect everyone. My decision weighs heavily on me, but I set my mind to it.

Dad says, "I ordered Sunday dinner. It won't be delivered till tonight. Give everyone my love and tell them we may have to move the night to Saturday. We'll have to see." Dad kisses me on the forehead. Ursula gives me a strange, maybe disapproving, look. She scowls as she walks up and suddenly hugs me. She smells of old-fashioned perfume, the kind old ladies wear. "If you need anything, Dear, just call." Her voice is husky and uncomfortable. Her hand taps clumsily on my back.

"Jazzy!" Hannah calls out as she comes through the door. I hear her from my bedroom, followed by the sound of feet stomping above me. My whole group is with her. Tiffy jumps up barking but doesn't go up the stairs. I jump at the noise.

"Is it dinner already?" I grab my chest in a panic. I

am apprehensive about seeing everyone, but I am also ready.

"Why aren't you answering your phone? It's been almost a week, Jazzy! Really! I have come by. We all have." Hannah's anger from worry boils over when she sees me. Grant and Aaron are setting up the food while I take my scolding. "Don't you have anything to say? We were so worried about you." Hannah is about two inches taller than I am. Her blond hair is up in a ponytail. I can't even look at her. I focus my gaze at the tips of Hannah's socks. Tiffy sits close behind me. Lance and Seth are quietly standing behind Hannah, watching me. "Jazzy, look at me! Why do you have your head down? What have you been doing?"

I raise my head. When my eyes meet Hannah's, tears start to well up. I drop my head again. Hannah softens her expression and voice. "Um, things have…" I started. Having him in the house was harder than I imagined. I couldn't think, and it is more embarrassing having Hannah question me in front of him. He doesn't even look like anything has happened. They all think he is the same person he was a week ago. I don't think I can do this. I can't breathe or remember my plan. It's making me flustered.

"Ursula took my phone." I feel a little bad lying to my friends, but I am relieved I don't have to explain anymore. I get my courage back. I should just stay away from him and not acknowledge him or ignore him.

"God, Jazzy, that woman is such a bitch. You need

to talk to your dad." I know Hannah doesn't believe the story; she knows something is bothering me. She opens her mouth to say something to me, but I guess she decides to hold off and watch for a while.

"You really OK, Jazzy?" Lance whispers in my ear. I push him away. Seth comes between us and puts his arm around me. I wiggle out of his touch. Lance pushes Seth in the chest. "Leave her the fuck alone." Seth smiles back at him.

"Or what, Lancey?" Seth says in a mocking tone. "Jealous?"

"Stop." I snap. I don't want any of them to touch me. I have missed my friends, but everything is different. The secret makes everyone seem distant. It is taking everything to contain my fear and anger.

Hannah sets up the floor pillows. She keeps looking at me. After a while, I widen my eyes. "Take a good, long look. It will last longer." We both break out laughing. It feels so good.

The night becomes normal again. Lance, Seth, Aaron, and Grant watch football. The boys yell at the TV and ignore us two girls. Hannah isn't saying anything about what happened earlier. I am glad that things are kind of back to normal. After dinner, cleaning up, and talking about the next day, which is the first day of school, I hold Tiffy, saying goodbye to everyone. I get ready for bed, feeling better than I thought I would. I will be strong and hold my head up.

CHAPTER 14

SUSAN

I see the boys walk Hannah home. I am sitting on the front porch when they get to the house. Grant hangs back, while Aaron, Seth, and Lance walk on.

"You want me to stay a bit?" Grant wraps his arms around Hannah, totally ignoring my presence. She places her head on his shoulder and her arms around his waist. I saw that it was such a strange night. I know Hannah wanted someone to talk her thoughts out with. I would like her to turn to me. She will in time, though we don't have much of that in this forsaken human realm, thank the goddess. It wasn't going to be Grant who Hannah talked to. He never wanted to talk about what Hannah was concerned with. I guess she would take being in his arms for a while, though.

"I want you to, but you are going to go with the guys." She wishes they had more time. "You smell good."

Hannah picks up her head and squeezes him. "Go on, Babe."

"OK." Grant kisses her and runs after the guys. He catches Aaron in a headlock. Aaron quickly moves out of the hold.

Hannah sits next to me. "Jazzy was so weird tonight. In fact, she has been weird this whole week." Hannah speaks slowly and thoughtfully, not to me exactly. Or do I hear her reaching out a little?

CHAPTER 15

JASMINE

As school starts, the small pack of us friends merges and mingles with the rest of the school. Lance, Seth, Aaron, and Grant are valuable members of the football team. No one can outrun, tackle, or catch better than the four of them. They have amazing skills in any sport, really. They are quickly engulfed with the varsity and junior varsity players. Freshmen players hang on the outskirts of the group. The team has already started practicing together. The cheerleaders are fast to join the pack. The school is not that big, so most people know each other. The first day of school is much more a catch-up day for the students, about what everybody did over the summer.

Hannah and I, and some of the other girls, last year planned carefully to have the same classes this year. Not all of them made it, but Hannah, Grant, Lance, Seth, Aaron, and I have the same homeroom. The morning is a blur with new classes, schedules, forms to fill out, and papers to organize. Class expectations are the theme of the day. Grant has made it outside of Hannah's class and is waiting with a smile when she walks out for lunch. The pack of six is now a small ocean of hungry teenagers for lunch. The whole corner of the cafeteria is full of talking, joking, and smiling friends. I love being around everyone.

"Jasmine, are you going to join the cheerleading squad this year?" Our friend Penny has been trying to get me to join since our freshman year.

"No, Pen, but thanks for asking." I wrinkle my nose and smile at Penny. I take one of her French fries. Penny scowls to herself.

"Hey, don't eat my fries." Penny gets upset. I know she is trying to be serious. I always try to joke with her. Penny feels like I must be brainwashed by our friends. Penny has known us as long as we have known each other. Penny's mother went to all the events that Hannah's and my mother would put on: card night, dinners, holiday parties, and the rest. Penny and most of the other kids grew up close. Penny was just as close to me as Hannah is. Their mothers weren't as close, but Penny always spent the night at my house. She did the same sport as me. I know she loved being part of us, especially when it came to Lance. I can't remember a time when she didn't like Lance. When my mother got sick, a lot of things changed for the whole community. For Penny personally, she had to watch Lance watch over me. The group broke up a bit during that time. He lived under my roof. Penny watched Lance fall in love with me. Penny works so hard at getting Lance's attention and keeps seeing him pushing closer to me. I don't care about Lance that way. The truth is I miss Penny. I am kind of hurt that she left me so easily. I don't want her to know what happened to me by our "friend." Somehow, I can't help but kind of pick at her.

"Why do you order a salad and eat my fries?" Penny snaps at me. I can't tell if there is any friendliness in her tone. I hope there is.

"Because I would eat all my fries and yours. At least now I get some veggies." I wrap my arms around Penny's neck. Penny slaps my arms away and glares at me. I grin back.

"Eat mine." Seth slides his tray over to me. My stomach feels tickly at his gesture.

"You are my most favorite friend." I joke with a wink. Hannah watches us from the safety of Grant's arms around her. She is picking at the slivers of carrot on her salad. Everyone is joking and having fun. I feel like I am in a safe place among the crowd. I have one moment of joy and the next of sorrow. The roller coaster of emotions is surreal, making the day go from super fun to sad, as if I can't make it through the day.

"Lance, don't you think Jasmine should do something?" Penny blinks her eyes at Lance, trying to hide her anger. "She doesn't do any of the activities ever. They want her on the track team. Field hockey wanted her too. She does nothing." Penny pouts at Lance.

"Penny, you can't force her," Lance answers her with a smile.

"Yep! Can't force me," I say beaming and cocking my head. I take another fry from Penny's plate.

"Jasmine, you're unbelievable. Stop it." Penny moves her tray out of my reach.

The girls and I leave and go to the girl's bathroom on the way to class. It is a kind of ritual; the boys go outside, and the girls go to the bathroom. Penny still seems frustrated from lunch. Not to mention the fact that we haven't talked to her all summer. Penny couldn't contain herself.

"Are you still leading both guys on, Jasmine? Lisa has liked Seth forever. Well, so have a lot of girls. I'm not holding back anymore on Lance, so you can say goodbye." Penny reapplies her makeup in the mirror while she talks to me as I sit on the counter next to her. I just stare at Penny.

I remember when Penny was with us all the time. Hannah says she has always been so selfish and worried about Lance. "What have they ever found so enjoyable about her?" Hannah would say. I don't see it that way. Penny still takes it all out on me. She blames me for the fact that her parents won't let her be with us. She blames me for Hannah's hurt feelings and the way Hannah lashes out at Penny. There are also a few of the guys who are not nice because they feel defensive. With everyone feeling sad and hurt, they all turned on Penny, and Penny on them. I feel for her, but she just sees me as the source of her alienation. Somehow this misunderstanding because of our parents has split this little family of ours. I am being selfish for always including her when it makes our group of friends fight. I also need Penny. My heart hurts when I see her. It makes the bad moments worse.

"When have you ever held back with Lance?" Hannah was checking her teeth on the other side of me. I turn to glimpse at Hannah through the reflection in the mirror. We wink at each other. We are quite the team.

"Shut up, Penny! Don't get me involved," Lisa says, rolling her eyes.

"I tell you all the time that I'm not dating anyone. Go for it." I unwrap a lollipop. I shoot my wrapper into the trash from my seat on the counter. Sugar is my only way of not falling asleep in class. There haven't been any school days when I didn't have a lollipop in my mouth. And now school has started, so I have the lollipops.

"Well, then, you should help me, Ja." Penny gives me a coy glance.

"Will do." I say, keeping the lollipop in between my gums and cheek. I jump off the counter, roll my eyes at Hannah, and shake my head, looking back at Penny and sighing loudly. Minutes later, all the girls tumble out of the bathroom and to their classes.

After school, Hannah goes to track practice, the boys go to football practice, Penny and Lisa go to cheerleading practice, and I walk home. When I was younger, I did sports. Every season was a different sport. My mom and dad would come to all my games. When my mom got sick, I just wanted to be with her. Now I don't know why, but I can't play any competitive games. I don't mind it though, and I go and support my friends.

There is a small group of kids that I walk with for part of the way. They smoke, drink, and have a bad reputation, but they are nice to me and accept me. I went to school all my life with most of them. I live in a small enough town to know everyone my age. So they aren't exactly strangers. I just don't usually hang out with anyone else. I don't want to stay at the school waiting for them. What if he thinks I am waiting for him? I don't want to feel this way. I just don't want to think about it. I have to think about building different friendships. It gives me something to do and takes my mind off everything that is hurting me. I don't tell anyone that I am spending any time with this group, mostly because it is just walking home or just in passing. No big deal. I kind of feel safe with them. We are all sitting in the park, catching up on what everyone did during the summer.

The boys and a few of the girls joke with me because of who I am friends with. I don't mind it. I have never hung out with any other school kids. We are all friends, but I have never spent one-on-one time with other groups. This is a first. Plus, I don't take those kinds of things to heart. I also know that Lance and the football team hate this group. After an hour or so, I say my good-byes and leave to go let Tiffy out.

The first week of school passed by without an incident.

I feel like everything that happened to me must have been a crazy dream. On Friday I tell the group I walk home with that I can't stay. They yell out, ribbing me as I walk off. I just wrinkle my nose and smile. Nothing can get me down today. It was all Hannah, Aaron, Seth, Grant, Lance, and I could talk about. Dad is coming home. I walk through the gate to the house. Tiffy is already outside. I run in the house.

"*Dad!*"

"*Oh*, Jazzy!" Dad wraps his arms around his little girl and lifts me in the air. He doesn't think his heart can take it; I am so happy. He smells my hair. I miss the smell of his cologne. "Oh, my girl." Tiffy comes running in behind me and is dancing on her hind legs around us two. "Let me see you. How was your week?" Dad tries to push me back so he can get a good look at me. I am not letting go. I start to cry. I have felt so removed from him and like I am growing into a different person since he has been working. I can't tell him, but having his arms around me makes it all feel better. I don't feel like I saw him the last time because I was still in shock. Dad holds me tight and kisses the top of my head. It is the best feeling in the world.

"Really. I think that is enough. It couldn't have been that hard to deal with." Ursula comes around the corner. I pull back in surprise and disappointment.

"Oh. Hey, Ursula. I didn't know you were here," I utter, feeling deflated.

"Clearly," Ursula mutters and comes up beside Dad.

"Why would you cry like that?" Ursula pulls her face back so that her chin almost blends in with her neck. I make a mental note to keep that image so I can tell the others. I am not going to let Ursula keep bugging me.

"Why can't I? Haven't you ever loved someone and missed them?" I try to mimic the face Ursula makes, pulling my face back.

"Oh, she is happy to see her pops." Dad chuckles.

The three of us sit down, and Dad tells us about his week. Somehow Ursula makes me uncomfortable in my own home. Dad and I don't laugh and joke like we normally do. Dad doesn't seem to sense the difference. Ursula is quick to point out what she finds lacking during my tales of the week—my mannerisms and behavior—and Ursula finds a lot of me to be lacking. After a few hours, I am feeling defeated and close to tears. I can't understand why my father doesn't see what is so clear to me. Just as I am about to excuse myself, Lance, Hannah, Grant, Seth, and Aaron come through the door. Hannah leaps at Dad, much to Ursula's dismay. Lance looks like he might do the same. The others hang back and wait for their turn. After more hugs and pats on the back, the now large group sits back down. Even though *he's* there, I feel safe with my father there. I still don't look directly at him, and I don't talk to him. No one seems to have noticed this whole week. The tone changes to what it used to be—laughter and loud talking, everyone trying to be heard. Dad suggests we order out. Ursula offers to make food and is quickly shut down.

"I am just trying to help. Alfred has been eating out all week. I thought a homemade dinner would be a nice change." Ursula sulks.

"The kids are just used to our tradition. I will take a rain check on that wonderful offer." Dad smiles and kindly puts an arm around Ursula's shoulder.

"Well, maybe I am too new for all of your traditions," Ursula fumes, pushing Dad's arm away. Hannah, the others, and I exchange glances at this behavior. Ursula sees the looks. "I see that I am not wanted here."

"Yes, you are! Please give us a chance." Dad gives a pleading look at Hannah and me for help.

"Please stay." I don't like my father to look this sad.

"Yeah, Ursula, please just stay," Hannah joins in. The rest of the group joins in on the plea for her to stay.

"Well, all right. If you all really insist." Ursula is smiling ear to ear. She has won this one.

The night continues with Ursula changing the habits and rituals of dinner. She moves everyone out to the table, putting Hannah and me on the stools at the kitchen island. We don't mind but are shocked that no one else seems to notice the exile. She is asking all sorts of questions and getting into conversations that are controlled and directed by her. She is heaping praise on the boys, who really seem to be enjoying her. The two of us are having a challenging time, mostly because none of the guys seem to notice or care how fake she is. But we have each other, and as we listen to the conversation, we have moments when we break into uncontrollable laughter. Each time it ends with a scowl from Ursula.

As the night comes to an end, Hannah and I clean up, and the boys walk Ursula out to her car, to her great delight. Hannah spends the night, and we text about how bad Ursula is to anyone who would listen to us.

CHAPTER 16

Mystic and Julie are starting to get ready for their trip to the regular world. They stay in a human city for six months of every year. Julie tries to hide her excitement. The love of her life, the man of her dreams, the vampire who is in her heart, is the most hated being in the village. This vampire is responsible for wiping out most of the humans in the village sixteen years ago. Thankfully, with Sung-Gi and Ryo's wedding and Shinan-Hua's defiance, the village's focus is off Julie.

Sung-Gi and Shinan-Hua know how Julie feels. The three always find time to sneak off together. They always have. Between them there are no secrets. Sung-Gi and Shinan-Hua know the way humans act and all about vampires who kill and drink human blood, and Julie compiles a list of questions the three are curious about. Darius has become fond of these question-and-answer nights when Julie first comes, and Sung-Gi and Shinan-Hua wait until Julie gets back and explains things as they have been explained to her.

CHAPTER 17

DARIUS

I look out the window to the night. My building is magnificent. It also is home to my favorite penthouse and state-of-the-art office. It is a haven for other businesses and residents, mostly my kind, but not my "father" and "mother," and they have never been here. Mother and Father are what I, for lack of a better term or long explanation, think of them. They are the vampires who made me and the oldest beings alive, although no one is sure about Mystic's and Susan's ages. Those are my parents. My mother is the mother of most all vampires. Susan and Mystic didn't change humans very often.

What I wouldn't give to be able to change my "family." I laugh to myself sourly. I did have a chance. Twice I could have chosen differently: the first time was in the arms of my vampire father, who asked me if I wanted to die quickly or live forever, and the second time was when the family split. Was it loyalty or duty that keeps me a slave to them? After over one thousand years as a vampire, most of my emotions are muted. My resentment for them is not one of the emotions that is muted. I will be the head of this family. I will be the most powerful vampire of all time.

The other emotion is my love for Julie. I cannot contain my love for her. Julie the human, Julie who spends half of her life living with the others of my family—the disloyal group. Disloyal to me and to our nature. They are spineless and shameful beings. Not even good enough to be considered vampires. I feel bothered that I have any type of gratitude toward them for caring for Julie. So I don't think about any of it until Julie is with me. Being as old as I am, I have learned to put thoughts out of my mind. Julie is safe with the other vampires. Elsabet and the other goody two-shoes. The despicable excuses for their kind.

I close my eyes. My first pleasant thought in five months comes to mind. Julie would be here soon. I hear the door open behind me and smell the human. I leave my thoughts and focus on the now. Taking in a deep breath, I smell who it is. Too much perfume and scented makeup. Bothersome. I wait for the human to sit down, then I move next to a young-looking woman who is a bit on the large side. I smile at her as I remove her special bracelet that hides my marks on her wrist. I have made a business feeding on humans, an empire with just this one part: feeding my directly chosen family members. I smile as I sink my teeth into her. Such a profitable business human vanity is. Her overly scented wrist quivered as she let out a moan of ecstasy. Ridiculous woman.

I have made a weight loss business feeding my kind. Bigger humans come to us to be fed off of. The body burns extra calories when there is excessive blood loss. The saliva of vampires has a healing effect. The results are that small amounts taken from the body on a regular basis by a vampire gives a youthful effect and increases weight loss. My company, Jabisell Weight Loss Division, takes between one to two pints of blood once a month from the client, along with their consuming a special diet pill that has been designed to enhance blood production. Humans don't know that but benefit from the side effects—youth preservation and weight loss. Special members get to have me drink straight from them or the other vampires of my company. The more they pay, the higher the position of the person drinking from them.

I think of how I love this fat, lazy country as I finish up with my client. She pays an additional $1,000 above the regular membership price just to have the pleasure of me drinking from her. *Not that I wouldn't pay more to have this beautiful, tan-skinned man touch me,* she thinks as I read her mind. Nothing special as usual, just lustful, dull thoughts. *What I wouldn't give to run my fingers through his jet-black straight hair that falls on his forehead.* She pays every five weeks like clockwork. In fact, I have all I can dream of eating coming through my door and paying me. I know most dream of me. I can read not only their body language but also their minds. The subtle and nonsubtle sexual advances are entertainingly humorous. They believe there's a promise of money, power, and fame if they could be part of my life. I find these lurid, fat, desperate humans pathetic. It is amazing I have the strength not to kill each and every one of these disgusting creatures. I laugh at the longing each shows at the intimacy of having me drink their blood. The spark in their eyes as they leave, hoping I will think of them. I wink and smile as they spill their stories and money at my feet. There are times I will lower their head on to me for a quick release of sexual tension. There is always something in the stories of everyone's life I can use later on, to trade or sell—keys to homes, leases to apartments, secrets to hold one hostage, and an endless supply of personal knowledge that each client shares in hopes of a glimmer of interest.

"Your next appointment is here, Darius." Nina, one of my made women and biological aunt to Julie, comes through the door. "You are looking so good. Come with me, and let's set up your next appointment and get you weighed in, Honey," she says to the woman on the couch who is in a slight daze. Nina's long curly hair bounces as she walks. Her dark, smooth skin has a glow from the fresh blood she herself just consumed. Nina is my most loyal wife. She does most of the dirty work, the henchwoman who follows through with threats that need to be carried out.

I have about seven pints into me soon enough. My thoughts drift back to Julie. My beautiful Julie.

The night continues with the feeding.

At 2:30 in the morning, I stop feeding, ending one business and jumping into another. I change my clothes and get ready for my meeting. This meeting happens once every three years. The aftermath is usually four months of separate meetings and an abundance of money for those involved. My father, Frank, and I sit with politicians, members of drug research labs from all over the world, members of major gangs worldwide, and other leaders above and below the law and their bodyguards and translators. Hundreds of well-dressed corrupt humans gather.

The hotel the meeting is held at looks like it is under renovation. As the cars drive through the plastic, it opens to a stunning marble drive up. Once you step out, you are greeted by a personal concierge who gives you a mask. The cream marble with copper veins leads a path into the main lobby, where it opens and covers the floor. The large entrance has no check-in desk. Some are led up the stairs, and some are led by their concierge through the door on the first floor. A very select few are led to an elevator and escorted three floors up. Each floor leads out to theater-type seats, and the third floor has one-way glass, so no one can see who is seated there. The seats are wide with tables between. Servers come to and fro with drinks, food, cigarettes, different drug samples, and a product list. Products from humans like passports and everything in between. Girls and boys dance on the stage with very little clothing while the members are all being seated. The cars are used from my company as are the drivers, food, women, and a few men. Everything is done secretly. These are the most powerful and ruthless. The background noise is deafening as people find their seats and get drinks.

The double doors on the side of the stage open. The energy in the air shifts. It is alive with adrenaline. Dealing with us vampires is always tricky and can cost you your life. A tall Frank, six feet four inches, walks through first. His gray beard matches his collar-length hair. His hair cascades in rough, bushy waves. He peers through thick, gray eyebrows. This imposing Nordic vampire sports a floor-length cape tied around the neck. With each step he takes, the sides of his cape expand and contract—more from his willing it to move with him. I know he enjoys the effect he feels it gives off. He is so old-fashioned. I hate how ridiculous he is.

I walk in behind him but not for much longer. I should be the lead on this. I started this whole empire. My father could never think this up and put everything into motion. I am much younger looking. I have the smoothest tan skin, the best of any 'pire I know. My hair is shiny, smooth, and jet black, not a touch of gray. I clench my jawline tight. It gives a stronger effect and keeps me from ripping my father's head off in front of everyone. I know I draw attention through my clearly dangerous beauty. I really am amazing to look at.

In close step behind me are my three lovely females. Nina, my office manager and most devoted of my lovers, is first. Her lovely, smooth face is the only vampire face that shows emotions. Her eyes don't leave me. There is no need to even check; I know she is focused on only me. She is the youngest 'pire. Tarissa walks beside Nina. She is pale to Nina's dark, she is blond to Nina's brown, and her hair is straight to Nina's curls. She is five inches shorter than Nina. Both are amazing beauties and my favorite, most creative bed partners. Behind them is still another beauty, Melissa. Melissa is tall with gray eyes and pale skin. She has straight black hair with a heavy bang. Melissa loves the power of being my wife. She pretends not to care about me, but I know it is for my attention. Trailing behind my devoted female entourage are another two male 'pires. The mass in attendance gets quiet, so still not even a clearing of the throat is heard. Each and every human knows the danger of standing out in the beginning of the meeting. We always make a point of showing who we are. Well, most know. There is always one, and we wait for it. The girlfriend of a senator whispers loudly.

"What is going on?" She annoyingly strokes her mink coat. I smile widely and nod to my wives. The senator slides his chair over, away from his girlfriend, as Nina and Tarissa arrive in front of the tender meal. The girlfriend screams as the two female vampires tear the girl apart. Chatter starts back up, and the meeting starts. An envelope full of money is given to the senator. He sits looking slightly uncomfortable sitting next to the bloody remains of his girlfriend. But the money will be more than enough to cover it up and pay off the people he needs to, to stage her death.

Agreements on prices for trafficking of all kinds, routes in and out that will not be monitored, drugs that need to pass regulation, and other items are talked about and agreed on. The meeting ends well. Only ten humans are disposed of, and companions are paid off.

CHAPTER 18

JASMINE

I walk home with the small pack as I have these past weeks. I am shuffling my feet while I'm in my own thoughts. Time has been flying, and a sort of routine is forming for me. I am not interested in their conversations, although I do find it curious the way they talk to one another. The guys seem to talk down to and make fun of the girls. The girls try hard to impress the boys, even though their feelings are hurt. I could never imagine any of my friends speaking that way to me or Hannah. But, then again, I never thought one of them could be the devil he is. I politely say no to offers of cigarettes or pot. But I kind of admire that they aren't afraid of authority or doing things that are illegal. I wonder why I even bother walking with them. They are so rude when they talk to me, picking on everything I do. Only one girl smiles at me sometimes when no one is looking. She seems familiar. I don't talk to the girls very much. I am a little intimidated by them. They seem so grown up and tough. None of them act the way my friends and I act. I wonder why I never see them in school. It is weird that I never noticed that not all the people are in the main part of school. I wonder where they are. There are a few I have seen in passing at lunch, always outside. I wonder how many other people go to my school that I have never seen. They seem to be a whole different species sometimes.

I'm lost in my own thoughts when one of these guys puts his arm around my shoulder. He snaps his head to the side quickly in order to get his hair out of his eyes. So weird, just cut your bangs. He has a joint in one hand. I'm scared that I'll get caught with drugs, and it is the strangest smell. But the encounter makes my stomach feel like a bunch of tiny bubbles exploding. Light and tickly, it feels wonderful, and the fear makes me strangely feel alive. I can't help but smile to myself. This is why I walk home with them; I rethink my stance on the group with a giggle. Hannah would probably never speak to me again if she knew I like a guy in this group or knew how he makes me feel. Everyone follows him in this group. Even the way he walks says he's in charge. He is a grade ahead. People are afraid of him and his group of friends, but I have always been impressed by him. I am a little embarrassed too. The whole group did things their own way and didn't seem to care what others thought, kind of selfish and inconsiderate. They were tough, and they accepted me when my friends weren't around.

We stop at the playground near my house. I sit on a swing. I watch my classmates, a group that others in school consider outcasts, with different eyes than I have seen them with before. They are laughing, chasing each other, dancing, and singing, and couples are kissing. Girls are wearing their high heels, makeup, and purses. Colorful, that's what it is, I think. Every move seems to be to show off for everyone else there, like a performance, a dance of calculated moves. It is exciting to watch. It is exciting to be a part of it. It has been different with my friends since—I try to stop thinking. I get up to leave.

"I'll be right back," the boy shouts back to his friends as he runs up to me. "I'll walk you home." He rewraps himself around my shoulder. "Jasmine?" Once we were out of earshot of his friends, his voice changes. I had never heard it sound like this. Kinder, more like a little kid.

"Um, yes?" My stomach is doing a strange dance. He smells different from my friends—smoke, cologne, and something I can't figure out all mixed together. Hannah and I pick out the boys' cologne, and Seth, Grant, Lance, and Aaron never complain. But now I think Hannah and I need to rethink this. This guy smells older, experienced. He shaves too, I think to myself. The boys shave too, but this just seems different.

"What's your deal with Lance and Seth? Are you dating both?" He walks looking straight ahead as he asks me.

"God no!" I am shocked. This is not a question I was ready for. Is that what everyone thinks? "They have been my friends since forever." I laugh a little. I've never thought about what people thought about those two besides Penny. It is weird to hear people talk that way about them. Part of me feels so defensive. But why should I defend any of them? Well, that isn't fair.

"Why are you laughing?" He is a little taken aback. He didn't expect me to laugh. He smiles.

"Kind of gross. They're family," I try to explain. I don't want to deal with any of them anymore, I think. Don't know why I feel so on the outs with them when I am around this group. I feel like they know me so well that they can see my shame.

"Well, let's not talk about them and not talk to them about me. They wouldn't like me walking you anywhere. Not that I am afraid of them. Just don't need the hassle."

"Nope, they wouldn't." I laugh again. At least someone else got the situation.

"What would you do if I liked you? Would you laugh at that?"

"No." I, all of a sudden, feel shy. I am not sure if he is joking or not. All the beautiful girls hang around him. They all look at him and show off for him. He definitely has a lot of girls. He couldn't really like me.

CHAPTER 19

HANNAH

Hannah is wiped out from track. All she really wants to do is go to bed because she is so tired. After track she had to do the things Grant likes. Now she is sitting on her bed trying to convince Grant to stay. She hates being alone with her father's girlfriend at meals. The woman watches everything Hannah eats. Hannah doesn't have a problem, but Susan talks about eating groups that helped her, hinting that Hannah should go. She always wants to have Hannah sit down to eat with her because Hannah's father never seems to be around. Grant is her only hope tonight. She doesn't tell him that she can't deal with it today. She has been feeling strange. Jasmine seems different. It's like she is pulling away from everyone. The guys seem different also. She doesn't know what is going on, but it is making her uneasy and sad. She just can't deal with Susan and the dinner thing. Grant and the others like Susan. Jasmine always takes Hannah's side and would never admit she likes Susan, but Hannah knows she does.

"Han, why are you so mean to her? She just wants to be your friend. She tries to be nice to you always."

"Grant!" Hannah cries out. "She thinks we are the same age. It's embarrassing!" She pouts, leaning her head on Grant's chest. She just loves the way he smells, the way his built chest feels, the way his arms wrap around her, accepting both the bad and the good about her. She loves his voice when he talks soft to her like now.

"She could be like Ursula. But she's beautiful and gets you all the things you want. She really cares about you. I can't stay, Babe," Grant whispers in her ear. He was going to meet up with some of the guys. He hates the vegetables and the salad crap they are always eating.

"Please—"

"Han—"

"Please, Grant, please." Hannah doesn't let up. Grant holds the pleading Hannah and finally gives in. Hannah joyfully passes on the message to her wannabe stepmother.

Lance makes it home. He doesn't like coming home to this house. It is always an anxious feeling. He never knows if his mother has started something with the neighbors or if she is passed out where everyone can see. Lance loves his mother but doesn't know how to stop her drinking and is scared that she will do something deadly. His mood is like the weather. He looks up and sees Penny sitting in the rain outside his house.

"Hey, Pen." He unlocks the front door.

"I've been waiting. What took you so long?" Penny stands up.

"What do you want, Penny?" Lance finally has a job. He just feels as if he needs to tell the others first. Feels like it would be a betrayal of sorts if Penny knows before Hannah and Jasmine. Hannah will kill him for sure; Jasmine will not care, which will hurt more. He scans the house for his mother, quickly concluding she's not home yet.

"I have been trying to talk to you all day." She walks into Lance's house behind him. He grabs a towel and gestures to her. She shakes her head no. He shrugs and starts to dry his hair. "You know I still like you, Lance. Why do you make everything so hard for me?" Penny delicately sits down.

"Penny, we are friends. We have been friends for years. Nothing has changed." Lance likes Penny just fine. They have been friends as long as the rest of them. They used to all play together. After Jasmine's mother died and Jasmine stopped doing sports, Lance noticed the girls didn't seem to get along. Penny has liked him since first grade. It's not that she's not great, he thinks to himself. Jasmine has always needed him, and he will always be by her side. "Are you hungry?" Lance pulls out two cups of hot and spicy ramen noodles.

Penny smiles; this is better than nothing. She sits down with him. They talk about the day and the teachers they have. Penny is careful not to mention Jasmine.

CHAPTER 20

MYSTIC

This is one of my favorite times of the month, but especially today. I will be leaving soon, walking the island by myself. Creation of any kind will communicate with me. Many don't know my origins; I have lived so long that I almost have forgotten why my beginning is not for human ears. I walk the deserted beach on the far side of the island. I am in the area my village doesn't come to. This is the area of the original beings of the world, the overseers of this land, the magic of the world, the reason this little land thrives. I watch the dolphins jump. Some have merpeople on them. Mermaids and merlads raise their heads up and shout out to me in the form of greetings. I lower in a slight bow to them and speak back in their tongue a return greeting. Queer little language they have.

Puppies run up to my feet. I turn my attention to the land. The young wolves, dragons, cats, and foxes become a small pond around me. These babies will grow and never interact with each other. But for now, they play and grow together. And the old mother gnome with her walking stick—she has a strange half dog, half dragon with her. This creature helps her keep all the small animals together. Behind her are giggly, happy fairies. The small pups and kittens nip at me, wanting to play. The mother gnome clicks her teeth, and the half breed is quick to round them up. They quickly refocus on the water and the creatures in the ocean. Bowing to the mother gnome, I continue, stopping briefly to greet the cute fairies. I must keep walking while talking to them, or I will be here all day playing with them.

We have strong whispers and shadows, so we can feel like we are one when we are together. Most vampires have whispers that aren't connected to our ultimate being. Every time a vampire kills a human, that human's whisper and shadow, a part of the human's soul, becomes one with the vampire. If the human is reincarnated, they seem soulless and, most times, evil. If that vampire dies, the soul becomes whole again, and the human can make up for their unbalanced karma. My soul is fully in me, as are fairies' souls. I am not fully vampire; I go back farther. We don't reincarnate. Humans have only a portion of their souls here on earth. Whispers are like drops in the ocean; you leave a tiny piece of your whisper every time you interact with anything. This means that when you have a relationship, a person has a tiny piece of your soul, like a tiny spider string. Humans are made up of relationships and nature. That is why it is important to be with good people. Makes you a better person because you have positive whispers encouraging your whisper.

My mind snaps back as I hear the trees talking to me. The air blows the messages to me. I greet the trees, shrubs, grasses, and flowers. As old as I am, as many times as I have seen scenery like this, I never stop feeling as though it is the first time. The beauty of nature is awe inspiring. I walk into the woods. I can feel the smaller beings. A tiny nisse runs out from the edge of the wood. There is a large farm that houses the cows, domestic deer, chickens of all kinds, goats, pigs, and a plethora of other animals. The farm is spread out. Nisses live to protect the farm. The fairies give and get presents from and for them, so the nisses of our island are happy. This tiny nisse is laughing and trying to throw pine pieces. A small gnome comes out laughing too. Gnomes are a bit bigger and wider than nisses, but they do look similar. Not a living thing would tell them they look alike. A nisse bite is poisonous. Plus, both are incredibly strong, and your personal home, pets, and belongings would be destroyed.

I carefully step around them and continue. Here I am at my truest self. The earth speaks to me as it does to everything here. I come to a clearing. The tall grass houses the most elusive creature alive. Most humans don't know of them—the cat people. They are not social like the fox or wolves. An adult can be by themselves their whole lives.

Those individuals who want some social life will maybe once a month come out and walk around interacting with each other. But these thin, tall, regal felines are majestic to visit with. Their speech is slow, and their movements are fluid and beyond graceful. It is captivating to be in their presence. I spend the next hour with these cat people. They are at the farthest end of the island. I am the only visitor, save the lonely male fairy, who hides here at times. Our conversation is easy and light, mostly about the wedding and how we think the next hundred years will go. After a polite conversation, we say our goodbyes, and I depart to make my way back to the village. I enjoy more creatures on the way home. This will be my last walk for the next six months. I don't mind the other half of the family, and I look forward to being with Mother. She is more fragile than any being knows. She is sick of living but afraid to die. Everything we have seen in this world since its conception has made her what she is. Some think she is evil. I think she is living as she was built to live. A perfect predator.

I see the youth as I head back. Those tiny ones we brought here are practicing punches with loud yells following each punch. I hear their whispers calling out for me to watch this or that one. Pride beams through each child's whisper. Not today, I whisper back. The older ones are working in couples. Sweat is streaming from them. Greetings are whispered to me. Each gives a slight bow and continues with their training. I walk down to my underground home as other vampires emerge.

CHAPTER 21

JASMINE

I am really starting to look forward to the end of the school day. Walking home with my other new friends makes me feel special, like I have a secret, something just for me. It's the first time ever I am not in a group of my family, who I love but who outshine me all the time.

"Why do you look so happy all the time? If I didn't know better, I would think the stories my cousin is telling about you are true." Penny slides her tray on the table between Lance and me. I heard about her showing up at Lance's last night. Hannah was mad and ready to confront Penny. I had to remind her that Penny is one of us. I am starting to understand how Penny feels—on the outside. Penny looks renewed in her determination to claim Lance after last night. She can have him. Lance said they talked until Bonny got home. I am relieved at the separation Penny provides. If she wasn't such a bitch, I would like the fact that she is sitting next to me. But she is being her usual bitchy self, glaring at me. This means she is going to start a small war. Why is it always me? Ready for her, I pull out my lollipop and put it on the side of my tray. Seriously, I wish Penny could realize I want her between us. Lance doesn't need to be all over my space, I think, slightly annoyed. Just about everything my guy friends do annoys me lately. I know part of it is having this secret, but what can I do? The whole thing makes me miserable, and being around them makes me miserable. His being at the table and in my life makes me miserable.

"What trouble are you starting now?" Hannah slams her milk box down. Penny has been going at me since the school year started. Hannah has gone after Penny just as hard.

"I hear your precious Jasmine is going out with the dropout." Penny smiles at the group with triumph.

"God, Penny." Hannah jumps up. "Why are you always so fucken full of yourself? Ugh, I just want to punch you sometimes. What has Jasmine done that you have to talk about her like that? Not her fault Lance doesn't like you." Hannah blows the front of her hair up with a fierce upward puff. I was always the focus of Penny's attacks. Hannah couldn't remember a time when it wasn't a problem. "Stop making shit up!" Even when we were little, Penny would tell on me at the drop of a hat. She always was out to get me in any way she could, or so Hannah has always assumed. I don't see it that way, but Penny is mad at me a lot of the time. Hannah says it is Penny's jealously because Lance doesn't like her.

"Jasmine?" Penny looks at me with triumph. My happy secret is going to be exposed.

"I walk home with that whole crew," I stammer, looking down. I am afraid to tell them. At this moment, I am embarrassed to know them. The shame of feeling embarrassed about another person makes me want to die. I am such a bad person for not standing up for them and for myself. Here, friends make the idea seem dirty. Their superiority makes me sick. Why are we so much better than them? What makes a group of people better or worse? I'm so sick of them.

"That better be all," Seth mummers under his breath.

"Stop spreading rumors, Penny!" Hannah sits down hard to make her point.

"Why are you doing that?" Lance asks Penny quietly but not quiet enough. Penny's face drops at Lance's reprimand.

"How is it always on me? I'm doing nothing wrong. It's Jasmine you should be questioning."

"Yeah, Penny, why? Do you think Lance is going to like you if you are a bitch?" the fuming Hannah continues. Then she turns on Lance. "Why do you egg her on? If it weren't for you, we wouldn't have to endure her."

"Enough, Han. Leave Lance out of this." Grant kisses Hannah's head. He's never really liked Penny.

I'm glad the conversation moved away from me. I tried not to laugh at Hannah, who keeps giving Penny angry glances. I am so thankful for Hannah. I feel bad for the many things I haven't told her.

CHAPTER 22

MYSTIC

"Breathe in." I walk around my kids—Ryo, Darton, Shinan-Hua, Sung-Gi, Raeleen, Kate, Julie, Bancroft, Lyesha, Anissa, Young-Sun, Jorn, Vincent, John, Nathaniel, and Kyong. I have watched these young ones grow into such fine adults. They would be middle-aged at one moment in history. If we can hold off fighting, they may all live long, lovely lives. "Breathe out slowly. Next position. Hold. Breathe in. Breathe out slowly. Next position. Julie, focus. Your mind is elsewhere. Keep going. Breathe in, then out. Next position. Stay together. Depending on each other without seeing is key. Your whisper bond is strong. Move together." Julie is not the only one distracted. The whole lot of them is focused on other things. "OK, this is not working. Sit where you are, and let us all do a group meditation."

I look up as the night is starting and see Elsabet watching me. Elsabet, one of my dearest friends, family, my family. I remember when she was turned right around 1,000 AC by her great-grandfather Frank. She and Darius followed Susan and me for the first hundred years like lost little puppies. After, the four of us were thick as thieves. Back then we all lived together. All us vampires stayed together. We fed off of wars and plagues. We were essential for keeping disease from wiping out the planet. Life was wonderful. Beautiful myths came from our existence. Homer was a friend of ours. We did get involved in the lives of humans we cared about or those from our ancestry line. But within our family, the four of us were inseparable for nine hundred years. Boredom and pride pushed Darius at times, but the three of us—Elsabet, Susan, and I—always found a way to pull him back in. During that time, we, as a community, were under siege, changing the way we were looked at by humans and the way we looked at humans.

The beginning of the end was in 1476 when we turned the greedy evil prince, Vlad Tepes. His boldness and villein killings brought us into a different light and started to cause a rift in the family in regard to what rights we have when it comes to the care of humans, who, for the first time, were attacking us. Then the stories came: Tate in 1600, John Policon in 1819, Whitby in 1890, and Sir Henry Irving in 1897.

Humans declared war on us. Many vampires were killed. Mother was enraged and swore to deplete the human population.

Elsabet stood strong in living the way we always had, being the protectors. Alexandra, a warrior from birth, after she was turned, stayed with Elsabet because of her beliefs. She wholly thinks her mission in life is to train and defend humans. Alexandra is the sole reason Mother allows us to exist. Not that she can take me, but we don't let anyone know. Mother and Susan know I am more than just a vampire; some may have guessed it. Tybalt and Perival followed. This brought many of the vampires who loved to party or were at one time famous. Two-thirds came with us. It was a slap in the face. I eased Mother's mind by promising to spend as much time with her as I did with the others. My decision to split my time allowed another thousand or so to join Elsabet and her large group. We took most all the humans who served us along. We built this paradise in less than a year. The underground city was quickly done first. Once we were able to settle down, the protectors of the earth started coming—dragons, gnomes, elves, pixies, and the rest. Humans started hunting all creatures they once cared for. Numbers were down too low. The earth screams out in pain, but we have to build their numbers up before they can go forth and bring the wrath to those who have abused the earth.

My lovely sister and friend started this and, in her way, will be the savior of this world. I just hope we can come back together soon as one family again. I look with pride at her. She nods, and I catch almost a smile. She must have been listening to my thoughts.

"Are we ready to try again?"

"Yes, Mystic, we are. We are sorry for wasting your time," the young group of humans yell out in perfect unison.

CHAPTER 23

JASMINE

Football season is an exciting time. Aaron, Grant, Seth, and Lance love the season, playing high school varsity and watching college and NFL football. Pops tries to get back early to see the boys' high school games on Friday nights. They practice every day after school and have games on Fridays. Sunday is dinner and football at my house. Seth and Lance have jobs. Penny and the cheerleaders practice as hard as the football team. They are the kings and queens of the school during this time. The band puts on a show during halftime. Every student goes to the games. It is a magical season for the school.

No one is paying much attention to me during this time. I like it like that. Last year I felt lonely if I wasn't with my friends. I would stay and wait for Hannah's track practice to be over. Now I sometimes feel lonely with them. The secrets are making me more uncomfortable around all of them. Seeing *him* daily, smiling and fooling everyone, is making me sick. I can't understand why I feel so mad at everyone else, but I feel ashamed, alone, and mad. As the football season starts to wind down, I worry about how I am going to keep my relationship with the group I have been walking home with. Hannah will figure it out soon because her field hockey practices will be over.

I try not to run out the door after school one afternoon. I love this time of day. I haven't seen the crazy group of new friends since Friday. Penny sees me leave. Sadly, I don't see her.

She takes it upon herself to try to ruin me. "I think something is wrong with Jasmine. I saw her crying as she was leaving." Penny rushes up to Lance, making her voice sound worried and out of breath, snickering to herself as she watches Lance and Seth take off.

The group I walk home with is sitting on the welcome wall in front of the school. The boy who gives me stomach flutters hops off the wall. I smile at him as I realize they are waiting for me. I am excited and scared. I walk toward him, trying not to show my excitement.

"Jazzy." I whip my head to see Lance is standing at the top of the stairs. I feel panic start to rise, and I feel hot.

"What?" I slow my steps. Why isn't he at practice? What should I do?

"What are you doing with him, Jazzy? How long has this been going on?" At first, I become consumed with guilt, embarrassment, and shame. Quickly it turns to anger and disgust at Lance, at all of them.

"Jasmine, you said he's your friend. Shouldn't he trust you? Not watch you like you're a baby." The boy walks up to me, talking too loudly. He snaps his head to the side quickly in order to get his hair out of his eyes. I can't help but smile at him. He takes my hand. I am thankful for the help, the support, someone on my side. Out of nowhere, Seth grasps his wrist. I look up at Seth, whose eyes don't waver from his face. Seth has never seemed so unflinching and angry to me. His eyes flash red. I shake my head. I am looking at a whole different person. My chest hurts for a second. I don't know why.

"Get your hands off her." I freeze everything but my heart that is beating so hard I can't breathe for a second. Seth's voice is scary. The two boys hold a stare. He holds my hand tighter and gives an eerie grin to Seth. I am still looking dumbfoundedly at Seth. What is this feeling? I want to cry. I want to run to Seth. I realize my hand hurts. He is squeezing to hurt me.

"We got a problem here?" A handful of boys come up from the parking lot. Kids circle around to watch.

"Let's go, man. We got practice. Careful, Jazzy. Get home safe." Lance comes up behind me. He speaks calmly to Seth.

"Oh, I'll make sure of that," the boy says as he jerks the hand Seth is holding out of his grip. "Let's go!" He starts to walk with me dragging behind him. I feel an odd sensation in my chest and knees as I look back at

Seth. For a second, I don't want to go. I want to go to Seth.

"Don't go with him, Jazz." Seth's voice is a whisper. But I hear it.

"Let's go. We're late." Lance claps Seth on the back. They turn slowly away from me. They walk back, passing Penny who is watching with a contented look.

I am silent the whole walk to the playground. "Are you OK?" He is sitting on top of the slide with me.

"Yeah. Thank you, and sorry." I feel stupid. The group of kids around them is talking about it and making fun of Lance and Seth. I'm not sure what to do. It's uncomfortable. The sensation I had is gone and replaced with a strange awkwardness. I don't want to keep dealing with all these feelings of being less than everyone else and being always told what to do, always letting everyone down. I just don't want to feel for a little while.

"Hey, guys, cut it out," he stands up and yells down. I can't believe it. It's as if he read my mind. He is so understanding. "Jasmine did an excellent job standing up for herself. Don't make my sugar girl feel bad." He grabs a six-pack of beer from the cooler they dragged to the park. "Drink this, my sugar girl." He passes me a beer and flashes a sexy smile. I don't think I have ever had a pet name. I smile to myself as I take a sip of my first-ever beer. I'm kind of cool, I think.

"Ew, disgusting." I spit it out with a pinched face. The whole group erupts in laughter. I feel stupid again.

"Jasmine." One of the girls who usually doesn't talk

to me sits down next to me. She has a lot of makeup on. I can smell it, smell her makeup. Black eyeliner, mascara, and a shiny, glittery nose are about all I can see, but I think it makes her look amazing. Her smooth skin is caked with an orangey-tan color. She has creases by her eyes, not from wrinkles but from makeup. "I don't like beer either." Her voice sounds so soft compared to how she looks. "Try this. Us girls drink these flavored drinks." She smiles through perfect lips and brilliant-white teeth. She pulls the tab off the top of a red drink and passes it to me with a wink. She seems so familiar, like something from a dream. I take a sip while looking at this girl.

The red liquid is sweet. "Oh, this is good." I smile back. The girl gives a quick glance at the group.

"Well, help yourself." With that she slides down the slide, goes over, and sits on a boy's lap. She gazes back at me with a friendly smile. I feel shy but incredibly pleased that she has acknowledged me.

"She's so nice," I say as I finish the sweet drink. "Could I have another one of these?"

The group yells out a cheer at my response.

Two hours later, I am yelling too. The world is spinning, and I am spinning with it. The wonderful red liquid is total freedom. I dance, sing, and tell stories to the amusement of the group. I have never felt so invincible. I laugh with them. The group focuses on another girl who takes over the dancing. I tell a story to the girl who gave me the red liquid, a story about a girl who gets beat up and raped by one of her best friends.

"I'm going to take her home. Now!" The girl who gave me the drink stands up and stops me midstory before I say who it is I am talking about.

"You're so pretty." The joy has turned to sadness. I feel a strange despair. I try to touch my new friend's face. Her perfect, painted face. Just so pretty.

"Jasmine! You must never tell that story again," the girl whispers. "He is a very dangerous person."

"Oh my god! Do you know—" The girl covers my mouth.

"Don't say another word, Jasmine. Do you understand me? Not another word." The group isn't paying attention, and the girl is talking in a low voice. She drags me home. No one seems to notice nor care.

My world starts to spin. I have to keep opening and closing my eyes to keep from spinning too much. I hear a conversation, but it isn't registering quite right in my brain.

"I wasn't sure who to call. Her dad keeps calling." The girl runs around nervously while Lance checks on me. I smell him. It is a familiar smell. Like home and safety.

"She is just passed out. Don't worry too much." Lance helps her relax. He tries to get me to sit up and to take some water and Advil. "Thank you for calling me. You don't have to stay."

"Lance?" I look up, opening one eye.

"Yes, Jazzy?"

"Ha! Why you are always around when I don't feel good?" I end my question by puking on him.

CHAPTER 24

Hannah doesn't like this time of year. Football is almost over, and everyone will be doing things together. She is stuck at track, which she loves, but sometimes she feels things are going on without her. Grant and his parents and Jasmine and her father's girlfriend will go to her meets and sit together, but the others don't. The boys work, and Alfred is gone during the week. Hannah never complains, except to her dad because he never comes either. She is feeling left out even before it happens. When she gets a call saying Jasmine needs her, she is relieved. Hannah calls the rest and waits for Grant to pick her up. When they see Jasmine, she is in the process of throwing up all over Lance. Hannah runs to the kitchen and grabs a roll of paper towels. She gets two sheets wet, runs to the mess, and unspins the roll on the puke. "Gross."

"Hannah banana fo fanna…" Jasmine starts singing and swaying back and forth.

"Yes, my Jazzy? What have you gone and done, Honey?" Hannah wipes Jasmine's face with the two wet paper towels. Hannah chuckles at Jasmine's antics. Seth works on the pile of vomit on the floor. Lance goes upstairs to clean up.

"He said I'm his sugar girl. I'm sorry you're not a sugar girl. What is a sugar girl?" Jasmine talks to Hannah while Hannah cleans her face. "He's not like our bad boys. Bad, bad, bad boys," Jasmine rattles on. She gets upset at the guys as she sees them. Her agitation makes it hard for Hannah to deal with her.

"She needs us to leave, I think. Make her take these when she wakes up," Lance says.

"Bad Lance!"

"Yes, Jazzy, I'm leaving."

"Good, because you are bad."

Grant kisses Hannah, and the guys leave. Hannah tends to the drunk Jasmine.

"Who is bad, Jazzy? Am I bad?" Hannah asks amused.

"No, but your mean, ugly Grant is very bad."

"What about Lance and Seth?" Hannah giggles.

"Lancey is bad, and Seth is so bad you don't even know." Jasmine is shaking her head.

"Aaron, he's so sweet."

"He's trying to trick you all. Awfully bad."

Hannah gets Jasmine in her pajamas. She holds her down to brush her teeth, get her to drink water, wash her face, and go to the bathroom. After getting Jasmine into bed, Hannah goes right to sleep, thinking it is too funny.

"Wait till I get my hands on that group." Seth punches the wall over and over. Grant stops him. Seth, Lance, Aaron, and Grant leave Jasmine's and go straight to the park. They are still there. Grant and Aaron stay close to Seth. His anger hasn't ebbed, and he is ready for a fight. They have one more football game of the season left, and they don't need Seth sidelined or even kicked off the team. Lance looks silly. He has on one of Alfred's T-shirts that's too big, but he doesn't seem to care. Jasmine soiled his other shirt.

"What have we here? It's the Jasmine cheer team," one in the group says, grinning. He walks toward the four of them. The rest of the group stand up and close in behind him. "Are you sad because you will always be on the sidelines while I'm in the game?"

"Shut up!" Lance comes to a stop in front of the group. Lance's voice is low and threatening.

"No, Lance, I don't have to shut up. I am not Jasmine. I am just freeing her from your grip." The boy walks up to Lance with a beer in one hand and a cigarette in the other.

"Paris, is that you? What are you doing with these losers?" The heavily made-up girl who gave Jasmine the drink freezes. "I didn't even recognize you when you called me to help," Lance says. "You don't do cheerleading?"

"No. Hanging with you guys ruined my life." She walks further back into the shadow.

"Just like you are ruining Jasmine's life." Dominik

stands nose to nose with Lance. Lance lands the first punch. Dominik is quick to recover and return the blow. Seth steps forward and grabs Lance up. Both sides erupt in vocal attacks and hand jesters.

"Not today, Buddy. Not today." Seth calms Lance down. He turns his head as they leave. "Hey, Dominik, let me give you some friendly advice. Stay the fuck away from Jasmine. She doesn't need a scumbag like you."

"Oh, you guys are the ones not keeping her safe from the devil among you. Did you know you have a devil among you?" Dominik yells after them.

"That would be all of you," Aaron shouts back.

"Don't answer to such stupid shit." Grant has his hand on Lance's back, guiding him away.

CHAPTER 25

JASMINE

"Leave me alone." I am angry and frustrated. I pull the covers over my head as my five friends stand around my bed, trying to get me up for school.

I know I have missed too many days, and Dad can't find out. But just one more day, I tell myself. I like the feeling of drinking. I am cool, funny, and free. It takes the edge away. I can talk and joke without feeling inferior. It seems like a magic liquid. Until the next day.

"Feels weird leaving Jazzy behind. Maybe I should stay here." Lance worries about leaving me.

"No," the group says together, each for their own reason. Seth is not going to let Lance get extra time with me, Penny won't stand for us spending time together, Hannah hates when we are not all together, and losing Lance for the day would be uncomfortable.

CHAPTER 26

DARIUS

After the meeting, which goes amazingly, I go to my second penthouse for the first time in almost six months. I love this place. I smile at the stuffed animals and pink accents everywhere. Alone in this special place, I loosen my tie and slide my jacket off. I pick up a pillow and breathe in deep. I can still smell her. I hunger for her, the way she moves through her world with her head in the clouds. The way she scrunches her nose when she is deciding on something. The way she sticks her tongue out sideways when she is concentrating. Julie makes me feel more human than I can remember. When Julie is near, I totally understand Elsabet and her do-good lifestyle. This penthouse is where Julie stays during her six months. I own the building and have this unit cloaked by special vampires. Some vampires have different abilities, like seeing into the immediate future; making people, things, and/or areas invisible to humans and vampires; or group hypnosis, having a whole area think it's raining on a sunny day. Mystic has all these abilities. She doesn't use them much, but she keeps herself connected to Julie during their six months away from Elsabet. Humans are evil creatures but nothing compared to me, if I am pushed, and the other vampires who Julie lives with. The worst is Mystic's family who are my father and mother. They want Julie dead and make no bones about it. Other than Julie, Mystic chooses to stay neutral and not use her abilities. Mystic had, at one time, used her gifts regularly, but her projecting into the future was part of what divided the family 120 years ago.

Before that, most all the vampires lived together. A thousand years ago, the main family members came together. (Perival is only about 816 years old, so he is too young to know the beginning of the end.) As a group they moved together, feeding from the wars and aftermath of conquests, slowly gaining members out of lust and greed. There were never too many turned. Babies born half human half vampire were not able to be controlled by vampires and were children of the earth and inevitably turned on the vampires. Fairies detest evil. Killing to eat doesn't bother them, but harming for fun throws the fairies into rages. A full-grown fairy can kill hundreds of vampires within an hour. Fairies live as long as vampires, if not longer. Over time fairies just killed vampires who came in their path, but because they are not hunters by nature, they would forget until they came across a vampire pod. Fairies were systematically killed off.

I drank lots of fairy blood. Because of that, I can get a human pregnant. I never would, and the vampire world condemned the birth of any fairies. We never want anything stronger than we are. We vampires encountered our first big resistance when Prince Vlad Tepes was turned. What his legacy left would name and change vampires forever. We used wars and plagues to cover death, to feed off the dying, or to raid villages. We were revered as gods, gods who decided who was to live and who was to die. It is the way the world needs to get back to. When I run this, I will make us gods again, me being the most revered god of all time. Some of us had favorite humans and would follow and protect even the descendants. This strengthens myths and folklore. But the prince and his revenge, arrogance, pompous attitude, and hatred were like no other. He led a few other vampires who agreed with his way to kill tens of thousands. A couple years later, he was captured and studied by humans, giving humans the first real knowledge about vampires and revealing the fact that we are not gods. After he was released, his behavior continued until the vampire family killed him and those who followed him in 1477, but the damage was done. Vampires, now named after a madman, went from gods to monsters almost overnight.

Around 1898 or so, Elsabet and her group—along with the one hundred fairies, werewolves, and another couple hundred humans—moved to this secluded island. Years of arduous work resulted in the villages underground and above. The village flourished. At first the division was not absolute, but now we are sworn enemies. The island also keeps safe the dying and scared gnomes, elves, trolls, nisses, dragons (not as big as humans imagine and very shy), and nature's other magical creatures. They live in the forest area and stay to themselves. These mystical creatures love the humans but are not crazy about how humans changed from caring for and worshipping them to hunting and destroying them and their homes. These small creatures don't trust the nature of vampires or werewolves, but this is the last safe haven for most of them, and their numbers continue to grow. Creatures like these are terribly slow to reproduce. So it may be many more years before we all get to see them again.

Werewolves have gone through many changes in their history also. Canis chibliersis divided, and Canis lupus became wolf. Canis armbrusteri and human created these creatures we call werewolves. The life span of around 120 years puts them at a disadvantage. They can raise their pups to conform to the vampire ways. When the divide happened, few werewolves left Elsabet. Those werewolves that live with Elsabet and that family are paired as protectors for and companions with humans or another wolf. They don't turn humans, so they are bigger and stronger than the ones I have. The flea bags are loved and treated with respect and dignity always, even by vampires. The few young fairies that were alive followed Elsabet. Fairies are about nature, and they know it would be a matter of time before they and all other creatures of nature were killed off with the other group. Fairies are born, not made. Ninety percent are female. They protect humans from unnatural, not born, entities, mostly vampires, but there are a few other things. Other than that, they have no interest in anything long term. They make no plans, eat when they are hungry, drink when they are thirsty, and pick flowers when they see them. They "flow." They have the ability to "push" nature. They can make a bud bloom and a small tree grow.

I smell Julie's scent. None of the history matters. I will bring glory to my name and Julie forever into my life.

CHAPTER 27

JASMINE

Having left school early, Lance, Seth, Hannah, and Grant are waiting in the emergency room lobby as Aaron and I come running up.

"It's going to be OK, Lance. Alfred is flying straight home." Seth pats Lance on the back. "I called him before we left school."

When the doctor comes hours later, the small group stands up to greet him. Lance steps forward toward the doctor.

"She's going to be all right, Son." The doctor's words are soft. "Lance, your mother is lucky. As I am sure you heard from the police when you first got here, your mother was behind the wheel of a friend's car. She hit a bridge and is lucky, firstly because nobody else was in the car and, secondly, because the car didn't continue over the bridge." The doctor's voice holds no shame or judgment. Lance looks crushed by guilt anyway. "Now, she needs to stay in the hospital for a while. She has broken her arm and leg. Lance, what I am worried about the most is what the alcohol has done to her." The doctor looks at his chart, but he has known Bonny and the group for their whole lives. He starts to get uncomfortable. "When is someone over eighteen going to be here?" This came out in a murmur.

"Alfred is flying home tonight." Seth steps up to answer.

The doctor finishes explaining what he can. Bonny's blood alcohol level was too high, so they could not do all the lab work they wanted, but she will be up in a room soon, and everything will get done in due time. The doctor reassures them. They sit back down to wait, feeling much better.

My phone rings. "Hi." I roll my eyes. "I am at the hospital now, Dad." I look around. "The doctor will fill you in when you get here, but she is going—" Seth grabs the phone from me and takes it out in the hall to continue the conversation away from me. I snort loudly. This is why I can't deal with them. He thinks he has some right to control me. His twisted mind thinks I belong to him. If he really meant it, he wouldn't let me feel this way. I am sick of feeling lonely and sad. Real rage starts to creep up in my stomach. Something else is under it too, something that hurts to think about, so anger covered it up—disgust and rage at how I am treated. Do they all know what was done to me by their buddy? I jump up. "I can't be here anymore." I start to walk out, passing Seth on my way out. "This is my fucking phone." I grab it from his hand. Seth stares at me in bewilderment. "Don't ever touch it or me again, asshole." I hate what I'm saying as I say it. But it hurts to be around them. I'm worried about Bonny but am ashamed that I was drinking alone. Like Bonny. I am becoming just like her.

I turn the corner and feel hands on me. He turns and pushes me against the wall.

"I have been letting you have your fun. You better start behaving, or I am going to pay you another visit, and this one you won't like." The small hairs on my face danced as his breath goes in and out. "I can't take much more before I break, so straighten up." With a final push, he stands up straight.

"Jazz, I'm sorry I grabbed your phone." Seth walks around the corner and stands there staring at us. "They got a room for Bonny and are moving her up. We can go and see her now. I won't touch you, Jazz. Just come on. Bonny will want to see you and Hannah the most." The look on Seth's face reveals he is questioning the strange scene he is looking at.

"Let's go!" He grabs my upper arm and directs me back to the group. Seth looks hard at his hands on me, and subsequently he lets go.

Aaron pulls Seth to the side later. "I found alcohol at Jasmine's house. That's why I was talking to her. She doesn't need to walk home with that group anymore, right?" Aaron is angry. He tells only Seth, not the rest of them. Too much else is going on. I hear him, though.

The teenagers help Bonny get settled in. I sit quietly by Bonny's bed. Even though Bonny can't move, I feel safest there. Penny joins the group after school. She has brought food for everyone and got most everyone's homework assignments. Once visiting hours are over, the group leaves. Lance stays and sleeps in the chair next to his mother. I sleep on another cot.

Lance and I wake up in the night. Bonny is in pain and is slightly shaking. Lance calls for the nurse. We find out that on top of her injuries, Bonny is now dealing with alcohol withdrawal. She is sweaty and hot. Out of sheer exhaustion, Lance and Bonny both pass out. I watch them sleep. My heart is so heavy; how have we fallen so far? When Lance wakes, he finds Alfred and Ursula at the end of the bed talking to the doctor in hushed tones. I must have slept also because I didn't see them come in. Lance is looking at his mom. She looks strange, but she is still sleeping. I know he is thankful for that.

"Hey, Son!" Alfred comes over. Lance rises and gives him a big hug. He seems to be trying to contain his emotions.

"Oh, Lance. This must be so hard for you, Dear." Ursula seems deeply concerned. Bonny wakes up, and she and Alfred talk. Lance and I go home for a bit. Neither of us talks. Both of us are in our own thoughts.

"Lance, we need to talk." Dad talks to Lance as we quietly listen. "Your mom is very sick." Lance lowers his head. "We are going to get her into rehab. She has to go, Lance."

"That would be great!" Lance looks up with hope. "How can we afford it?"

"You let me worry about that." Dad told me earlier, but had no heart to tell Lance, that he found Lance's father and talked to him. Lance's father said he couldn't go back. He couldn't face his family. In the end, he gave money and promised to pay for rehab and hospital bills. "She'll be moved to a rehab tomorrow. The thing is I can't keep your apartment too, so I was thinking of moving you into the house." Lance smiles. "Your room will be my office. We'll move my stuff out."

"No, sir. It's fine in there. You can keep everything the way it is." Lance tries to act cool, but I can see he can't stop grinning. He loves Dad's office stuff. It smells like him. Lance used to pretend Alfred was his father and this was his bedroom. We all know this; maybe Dad doesn't.

"OK. I was hoping you would say that because I've talked to your landlord." Dad grins, then talks as if I am not there. "Jasmine seems off lately. It will be good for you to keep an eye on her. I have to shove off today, so I'll leave it up to you kids to get what you need from your house. A company is coming Wednesday to pack up everything for storage. Make sure you get the things that are important to your mom too." I can't believe they are talking as if I don't exist. "Do you think you can sleep there tonight?" The hospital staff wants Lance to stop sleeping there.

"Pops, that would be great, but maybe I should be here one more night with my mom."

"Son, you have been here almost a week. I think you need to go back home tonight." We all see how dedicated Lance is. It has been over a week, and the boy has spent every night beside his mother. The alcohol withdrawal had gotten so bad that the staff moved her to a private room and sent Lance home. When the worst was over, Lance returned to his spot, leaving only for school. Dad sent him to go home this past weekend while he was home. All of us have been there during our free time, but Lance left only when Dad was there. "I can't force you to, but she has to do these next steps on her own, and it may be better for you to create some distance between each other. The place she is going to go to is in California. She won't be back for three months. Almost the whole summer break. Both of you need to prepare yourselves."

"Hmm, you're right," Lance answers, shaking his head in agreement. "OK, Pops." Lance is admitting he is wiped out. We all see it.

After Dad and Ursula leave, Penny jumps up and stands with fists in a ball at her side. Everyone in the room stares at her. "I can't grasp how unfair what I just heard is. Everything falls into Jasmine's lap. Why should she get Lance also? She never has to struggle for friends. I have to have a trainer for every sport I do, a tutor for schoolwork. I have to work so hard for everything, and no one ever stands up for me. No one sees how hard it is to be on the top. I have to work the hardest to be noticed by Lance, and I am not going to give up. Not for stupid Jasmine. I hope you don't think this means Lance is yours!" Penny spits out at me.

"What the hell do you mean you are moving back in that house?" Seth sounds like Penny. "How the hell is that going to work?" Seth is enraged, and his voice is breaking as he tries to sound kind. "Maybe all this stress has unglued your brain."

"Nah, man, I'm going to move things forward with Jasmine. If anything, everything has made my brain clear," Lance declares. We all stare at Lance. I don't know what the hell is going on. I am so not interested in Lance. He is my brother. Gross. Can't say it now. Why are we talking about all this with Bonny having so many problems?

"Not going to happen. Sorry, bro, but I can't let you do that."

"Not asking permission, Seth." Lance is not looking at anyone but Seth. If he looked at me, I would signal him to shut the hell up. "I hope it won't end our friendship, but I won't hold back."

"I've been thinking about your feelings, Lance. I warned you. I will not give her to you, and I will not back down." The boys are standing now, eyes locked in battle, when they hear a scream. Penny is bright red. Her anger is obvious.

"We aren't talking about any of that until Jasmine and I have a talk on our own. I need all your help. Got to move my stuff in tonight."

I shake my head. I want no part of this. I now don't

want Lance to live with me. How weird is that going to be?

"Oh, I'm going! Not going to help. But I'm going," Penny states with eyebrows high and head slightly shaking. I don't blame her. How cruel for Lance to say all that in front of her. I am starting to understand why she hates me.

The kids stay with Bonny for dinner and head out to grab what they can from Lance's house. I am a little bothered. First, because for some reason Seth makes me uncomfortable lately. I feel flush and want to know what he's doing when he's not with me. Now I know Lance is making life difficult, and I can't yell at him because of his mom, my Bonny. It makes me angry that he is making choices for me, for some reason. My new group of friends doesn't seem to care one way or another that I am not around, and it makes me feel left out. I am deep in thought when Seth grabs the heavy trash bag I am carrying out of my hands. Shocked, I peer up at Seth. That strange sensation comes over me again. I become shy.

"Jasmine, I'm not sure what is going on. I got to say something. Last week when I saw you with—"

"It's not what you think."

"Don't worry, Jasmine. And the whole thing with you and that whole group and that waistoid?"

"Oh, yeah, we are just friends, Seth. You know that."

"Yeah, that's what I figured. Anyway, Jasmine, I like you. You know it, but I have never said it straight to you. I want us to—"

"Jasmine, we have to talk." Lance pushes between us, interrupting Seth with a shoulder shove. Lance is lugging two large bags and has a backpack on as well. "Tonight, when everyone leaves and it's just you and me." Lance says the last part looking at Seth. He lumbers forward.

"Um, what were you saying?" I say to Seth. I hope we can talk more; Seth can't seem to regain his thoughts. This wasn't going to be easy. I feel a little disappointed.

The group stays late. Penny sets to work making Lance's bed and putting his clothes away. She is bossing everyone around, so before long she is the only one in his room with him. The rest of us are downstairs. We get sick of Penny, and she is simply fine with that. Lance is thankful for the help and can't stop yelling out about how we flaked out on him. Seth is playing with my hands while Aaron, Grant, and Hannah play cards. I'm not sure what this all means, but I like it. Hannah smiles approvingly at me. I smile back at her. My hand tingles where he is touching me. My heart flutters, and my stomach spins. I can't get rid of the goofy grin on my face. The others notice, although they pretend not to see. Penny comes down the stairs to get a trash bag and sees Seth and me. She is thrilled. When she goes back upstairs, Penny starts talking about how good Seth is for me and how cute we look at the table together. Lance quickly slams the drawers closed, runs down the stairs, and tells everyone to go home.

The next morning, Seth arrives at the house before

anyone else gets up. Letting himself in with the spare key, he sets to work on unpacking the food he brought for breakfast. He is going to celebrate. This is going to be the first official day. He is going to ask me out this morning. Yesterday was amazing. My hands were so smooth and warm in his. I think I feel the same way Seth feels. *I just can't wait to see her this morning*, he thinks as he smiles to himself. Last night he couldn't sleep at all, thinking about me. We texted late into the night. There is a tiny part of him that was hoping I would be feeling the same and would be up with him this early. That way he could have asked before everyone got up. He is making breakfast when Lance gets up. Seth calls for Tiffy who quickly comes up the stairs. He feeds her and lets her out while Lance eats. He has a special plate for me. Every nine minutes, they hear my alarm goes off, followed by a huge thump.

"What is that? Is Jasmine going to get up?" Seth eagerly glances at the stairwell. He is going to be sure I see his face before Lance's. Plus, the food is getting cold.

"Ha! That's her hitting her alarm. I'll get her." Lance laughs at Seth's expression. Lance is used to the morning sound of me and my alarm. I have never been one to get out of bed easily. Seth has been expecting an argument or at least some smart remark about his being here so early. Seth suddenly remembers that today Bonny leaves. His excitement and good mood drop to sorrow. He must wait to hold my hand again. His whole plan must be put on hold. Whatever is going on between them and me doesn't stop them from being best buds. He can't hurt his friend at a time like this. Seth has always helped with Bonny. All the guys have really, but for Seth it has a different meaning. Seth has been raised by his father who is an alcoholic also. His father differs from Bonny. Seth's father tends to be cruel when he drinks, which is every day. Bonny never seems to mean any harm. She's like a lost, lonely puppy. You want to look out for her. Now she was leaving for three months. Seth feels bad for Lance and even worse for himself.

"You OK, man?" Seth says before Lance goes down the stairs. Seth is unable to do anything to help, partly because he's now upset himself. "Want to go to the hospital and see her off?" Seth tries to shake his own feelings off, so he can be there for his friend.

"Lance, what did my dad say about today?" I forgot it is an important day as I come running up the stairs still half asleep and with a stubbed toe. "Are we going to the hospital?" I stop in my tracks when I see Seth. I try to smooth down my unruly hair. "Hey, Seth." I get a giddy feeling inside. My face breaks out into a huge, uncontrollable grin. I look at Lance, and my smile falls. Lance seems crushed. I can't blame him.

"Not allowed to be there," Lance whispers. "Thanks man, I'll be right back. Got to finish getting ready." Lance goes up the stairs as Penny arrives. Seth turns from me and starts to pick up the food except for my plate, which I sit down and eat as fast as I can. Then I leave Seth and Penny in the kitchen and go to get myself ready. Penny is a bit bothered that things went on without her there. She is careful not to say anything because she doesn't want to upset Lance today, but she glares at me every chance she gets. I just hope everyone will be as thoughtful to Lance today because of everything going on with his mother.

The walk to school is sobering. Lance is lost in his concern for his mother. The rest of us are worried about Lance and Bonny. Seth walks far away from me. I can't understand what happened between yesterday and today. I try to figure out what I have done.

The week is a long one for Lance. We hear nothing about his mother. He calls the contact person every night, who tells him everything is fine. Dad reassures him every night that she is doing OK. Dad prepared him for this, but all of us can see he's having a hard time not being able to hear it from her.

Lance and Seth are both working during their free time. They both got jobs at the local sports store. Seth always works in between seasons and in the summer. His father tends to not be consistent with giving him money for school and other things he needs. Seth doesn't make that much, but it is enough to get himself food and clothing and to pay for the extras that come up in his life. Lance is now doing the same. He doesn't want Dad to pay for everything, and he wants a bit of extra money for when his mother gets home. I am too wrapped up in my own situation to notice what anyone else is doing. Hannah still is doing track. She texts me all the time. I know that because everyone is busy, she gets a lot of time with Grant, which she just loves. They spend time at Grant's house, so Hannah doesn't have to deal with her father's girlfriend. Grant's house is big, and his parents are so nice to Hannah. She always loves going there. Grant never seems to want to be there.

Seth doesn't even look at me anymore. I have no idea what I did, but it reminds me of how finicky my friends are. My feelings are hurt, and I am mad at him. My group of new friends keeps my mind busy. I am drinking with them more, and I always have fun. It seems they always have something they are laughing about. Some of the other girls have even warmed up to me and are saying hi to me in school. Hannah couldn't care less who I talk to, but Penny uses every bit of this she can, always wanting to know why this one says hi and if I know that one. But they give me something to look forward to each school day. As the weeks go by, I am once again distant from my friends. Penny seems to have taken my place. Now she walks up front and is at the house every Sunday. Penny and Hannah are setting the table for Sunday dinner. Lance, Dad, Grant, Seth, Aaron, and Ursula are catching up on everything. Dad is giving the doctor's report on the progress Bonny has made with settling in. I am lying my upper body down on the table. I am in the way of the girls but make no attempt to move. No one notices me. I now find Sundays the worst since Lance has been living with me.

Penny and Hannah are chatting about their weekend.

I give loud groans when asked any questions. Hannah smiles at me, "her pouty friend." Hannah doesn't care. She now has had tons of Grant time and is giddy. Not having me around is working for her. Penny spends most of her time around Lance's work. She feels like she has gotten closer to him. Dad ignores my mood. "I know things must be hard without me there" is all he can say. I guess that is why he doesn't want to give me a hard time. Ursula has also noticed my moods as of late, but when she says anything, she is quickly shut down. She says it must be a teenage thing, but her face shows she doesn't like it at all. I snap at Ursula every chance I get.

Finally, Lance gets to talk regularly to his mother. He relays all the messages. Bonny mostly worries about me. She has always had the softest spot for me. I used to want to be around her, but now I just find this burdensome and bothersome. I am short with my words when we talk. Bonny apologizes for what she has put everyone through. I feel like we have switched places, and I am ashamed and don't want to think about it. I hate thinking about it. Lance never seems to get upset with me, even when I know my behavior gets bad. Penny can't believe and continuously talks about how bad I have become, and no one seems to care. Seth has been cold to me since Bonny left, and I have decided I am just fine with that. I have all but stopped talking to all of them, except for Hannah. If Hannah remains so bubbly, she may be next, I think sulkily as I make a snarl face at her.

Dinner is full of chatter, except for me; I don't speak

and only have three bites before Ursula reprimands me for having Tiffy on my lap. I quickly excuse myself and Tiffy and go down to my room to be miserable by myself. This misery is consuming my life. I don't know how to stop it or why I am so sad. I don't know what I did to Seth. I am still in my room when Ursula goes home. No one comes to check on me. I am still in my room when Dad leaves for the week, leaving my well-being in Lance's hands. I cry out of frustration and sadness. I hear my friends talking and laughing. No one cares that I am sad. I feel so removed from them. It seems I'll never get back to where I was with them. It is so lonely. My whole body hurts. I think my chest is going to break apart. Why won't Seth talk to me?

Lance comes down to check on me after everyone leaves. I am half asleep. My face is puffy. Tiffy is curled up against me. Lance looks at me with pity. He brushes the hair off my face. I am too exhausted to push him away. I don't care anymore. It is all just too much in the way of emotion and being unloved.

"Why are you doing this to yourself?" Lance asks as he rubs my head. Tears well up again. I can't talk. I break down and cry most of the night and pour my thoughts out to Lance, not the Lance who likes me but the Lance who has been my best friend and brother all my life. I cry out my loneliness and lost heart. I plead for life to go back to the way it was. There is only one thing I keep from Lance. It is the one thing that's tearing me apart.

Lance doesn't speak of it again. The next day, as the whole troop sets off for school, to everyone's shock,

Lance closes the front door and takes me by the hand. I shake my hand free and widen my eyes. I quietly take my new spot I have created these last few weeks in the back of the group, with Penny planting herself up front. Lance grabs my hand again, and I can't shake free from it. "Why should I give up on you? Why should it be Seth and not me? Jasmine, you are so lonely, and I am not going to let you keep feeling that way." I have no idea why Lance is acting like a lunatic. Why in front of everyone? When did I act like I want Lance? Did he not listen to me? I can feel panic rise inside. Penny can't hide her disappointment. Seth tries to ignore us and walks looking at his feet. Seth sulks the rest of the day and talks to no one.

After school, Lance skips track practice. He grabs my hand and starts to walk with me. My group of drinking friends stops us and makes a half moon around us.

"Where are you going with my sugar girl? Where are your besties?" one of them snickers. The others join in. One girl turns to leave. She flashes a look of fear to me.

"She's not your anything. And she's definitely not your sugar anything." I feel silly for having ever liked that nickname. In this moment, it sounds stupid. I wish we could just leave. I just want to go home. I am so embarrassed, and I don't know who is embarrassing me—Lance or this whole group I thought of as friends. My mind is whirling while the boys are arguing. Before I know it, their words become fists. Lance and one from the group are fighting. Lance had the upper hand and is landing blow after blow to the face. The others join in. Lance loses his footing and is hit in the back of the head. Arms come around me as I yell and try to stop it. A large boy is holding me back as fists and legs are smashing into Lance's body. The bloody boy who Lance started the fight with is stomping down on Lance's ribs. Lance is unable to get up. The frenzied boys laugh, howl, and beat at Lance until I break loose from the arms that are holding me and cover him with my own body. Lance is bruised and bloody but OK. I yell at the mob who laugh at my attempt to defend Lance.

"You shouldn't have picked him," they shout back at me. Fear grips me, but I still cling to Lance. Lance is working to get his feet under him. The group moves on, shouting jeers. Lance is now standing, but his ribs hurt. After they leave, I call Aaron. Aaron comes, and we get Lance back to the house. As we clean him up, we call Hannah, Grant, and Seth. Later I call Penny, to everyone's dismay. Lance refuses to go to the hospital.

"Do you see what you've done?" Penny starts right in on me. I can't stop shaking.

"Penny, you wouldn't be here if it wasn't for Jasmine." Hannah is too worried to fight. The group sits around Dad's office, which is now Lance's bedroom. I am still checking Lance's bruises and icing his face and side. The guilt is breaking me inside. I busy myself so as not to have to talk to any of them.

"I'm so sorry, Lance," I say for the millionth time. "So, so, so sorry."

"I'm fine, and Jasmine saved me. It's not her fault," Lance says with a wink from his swollen bruised face to me and quickly cringes in pain. I can't bring myself to smile back. I may never smile again. What I wouldn't give to do this whole year over.

"Yes, it is. She has been having those losers over and drinking with them," Penny says. The room gets quiet. I put my head down. Lance tells them he knows.

"Even after we told you to stay away from them. You're still drinking?" Seth shakes his head. "You know what drinking has done." He can't stand the idea of drinking and especially me drinking. He can see how upset I am. "Wait till I get my hands on those assholes."

"Now you are going to lead Lance on again?" Penny shrieks out. "I can't stand Jasmine helping him. I can't stand her touching him." Penny rips the ice out of my hand. I sit down as far away as I can.

"Penny, I think you should go." Lance's voice is harsh. "I'm not about to listen to you start in on Jasmine. I still can't believe how brave Jasmine was to shield me." He grabs the ice and reaches out to give it back to me. I go back to icing his face.

"No, Lance, I won't leave. I have every right to be here too." Penny crosses her arms and is finally quiet.

"Jasmine?" Hannah's voice is soft. "Why? Why didn't you talk to me about any of this?" The hurt in Hannah's voice rings out. I gaze into Hannah's face. I have been so worried about what was going on that I never realized how I was shutting Hannah out of my life. It wasn't her pushing me away.

"I'm sorry, Hannah. I didn't know what to say. I hated not telling you, but I didn't know how to. I didn't want to lie to you." I return to working on Lance's bruise. I can't bring myself to look into Hannah's eyes again.

"But you did."

"Yes. I'm sorry. I apologize to all of you."

"You can talk to me about anything. Don't suffer alone." Hannah walks over and hugs me. I am again brought to tears. I wrap my arms around Hannah. It feels so good.

"I don't know if I forgive you," Penny says. "I am sick of Jasmine screwing up and everyone forgiving her. What makes Jasmine so great?"

"Leave, Penny," they all say in unison.

After a quick talk, we decide not to tell Dad what has happened, against Penny's protests. Seth, Aaron, and Grant are beside themselves and plan to get back at the group that beat Lance immediately. Lance tells them to leave it and not do anything. It takes a half hour before the boys agree to leave it. After everyone leaves, I check on Lance, who assures me he's totally fine and goes to bed.

CHAPTER 28

SETH

Seth's, Aaron's, and Grant's attitudes change as soon as they walk out of the house. Retribution is the only thing on their minds. They call their team members on the way to drop Hannah at her house. They meet up with those who can come out and hunt down the group. The whole group is ready for them. They know they were going to come with everything they have.

"You are going to pay for what you did. But I am warning you, if you go near Jasmine ever again, I will kill you," Seth growls.

"Oh, I'm not just going to touch her—" One of them starts to get his words out, and Seth's anger erupts. With that both sides attack each other. Seth releases his anger on whoever is in front of him fully, the already bludgeoned leader of the group. The one who fought Lance is not able to recover and is on the ground quickly. Aaron has one pinned up to a tree and is giving him body shots. He is returning the blows, but he cannot match Aaron. Grant is more evenly matched until a teammate helps Grant out. Seth is moving through boys, his fists slamming into whatever comes his way, but he still can't stop his anger. He is knocking them down as fast as they come to him. The fight is long and takes its toll on many. But in the end, there are more football players, and the team is in peak condition and still standing.

The next day at school, there is a large number of boys from the group and the football team who have bruises and puffy faces. No one talks about it again. The matter is over.

CHAPTER 29

JULIE

I hold the phone to my chest. I love this time of year. The weather is colder, not like on the island. The village is cloaked from the world, so the air is never too hot or too cold. Not like here, outside the secret world, where I spend half the year. I can see my breath when I roll the window down and blow out. It puffs out in a blob-like mist. It's a beautiful November night, and I am on my way to the big city. The cool air brings with it the promise of half a year spent with my love, my everything. I feel uncomfortable talking about him. His family caused so much destruction to those I love. Sung-Gi is my confidante on this matter. She never judges me. Shinan-Hua is, to a degree, but as she gets older, she starts to feel the way the rest of the village does and makes me feel bad. The whole situation sometimes makes me feel lonely and alienated at times. I look at his text again. It tells me to keep alert and to keep Renton as close to me as I can. Renton is snuggling in wolf form against my leg. Renton is hoping just to keep "this silly woman" warm. I know he can't stand this time of year. Every creature is an enemy to him. There is no place he can get help from if things go bad. He is not scared, but he doesn't like being away from his family and being so isolated, not to mention keeping me safe from everyone. The wolves here are different from our wolves, scrawny with no self-pride. They are a disgrace to werewolves. Renton shivers a little and curls closer to me. I keep rolling down the window. I smile, not caring if I am cold. I am going to spend six glorious months with Darius. I hug my phone and roll the window down to feel the breeze in my hair. Mystic smiles lovingly at me.

Mystic is the only vampire who likes our relationship. She doesn't see good or bad. Well, most 'pires don't think in those terms, and neither do the villagers. Just humans from the regular world. My village has been at war with this side of the "family" since around the 1900s, which is all I hear and think about. Mystic, Susan, and I are the only ones who straddle the two families and their very different ways of living. But Susan has disappeared for five years. I couldn't imagine it any other way. I wish I could bring Shinan-Hua and show her the different types of people living any way they choose, the energy of the city, day and night, the stores, restaurants, clubs, subway, and the people on the street. Everything that's trying to attract your attention day and night. Shinan-Hua would love it as much as I do. Sung-Gi would hate it, but I would still like to bring her. This is Shinan-Hua's world, I think to myself.

I push the reality that Darius and his family would kill them on the spot, in the most painful way, from my mind. I love Darius and know what he is and what he enjoys doing. I have never pretended I don't know. Part of me is excited by the fact that I sleep with danger. I have seen Darius kill and feed. He shows extraordinarily little emotion. None of the older vampires I know show emotion. And I know a lot! I laugh to myself. He does get jealous when it comes to me, so much so that seven vampires, over a dozen men, and three women have died on the spot from making advances toward me, disrespecting me, and putting their hands on me. I quickly push the thought from my mind. I feel uneasy with the fact that part of me enjoys that he acts this way. I feel like I am someone special.

The next evening, I open my eyes to Darius watching me. Time is a bit different. Darius can't handle sunlight as long as most on the island. So I stayed up and watched the sunrise with Renton, then went out for breakfast before lying down next to Darius at around 11:00 a.m. The penthouse has special windows, blinds, and curtains for daytime. I slept straight through the day. I never dream when I am with Darius, and I always sleep without waking.

"Mmm, good night, my love." Darius leans down and kisses me on the forehead.

"Hi, Babe! What time is it?"

"Five in the morning. It's still early, but I want some time with just you. Can we get rid of your flea bag just for one night?"

"Darius! You promised me you would be nice to Renton." I pout, then giggle. "I have to pee." I cheerfully jump up and walk toward the bathroom.

"We have to see the family." Darius sits on the edge of the bed and looks down at his feet. I freeze for a moment, then continue to the bathroom.

"I don't want to," I quietly state as I return.

"They know you are here. We must."

"Please, Darius!"

"Let's go eat and feed your flea bag, then we will go visit. Hopefully, they will leave you alone and eat Renton."

"*Darius!*"

"Sorry. Sorry, bad joke. Come here." Darius wraps his arms around me. He hates bringing me to the family as much as I hate going.

CHAPTER 30

JASMINE

Bonny is doing well and calls often. I talk to her. Bonny was the one to go to and tell your feelings to when we were younger. She never told on us and never held it against us. Now it was the same. I tell Bonny that I was attacked. I leave out the rape part and who it was. I tell Bonny how much I care for Seth. I tell Bonny about the group that I thought of as friends, about Ursula, about drinking, and about the way it made me feel. Bonny tells me stories about my mom at my age. She gives advice that she thinks my mom would give me, and she gives me advice she thinks will help. For three nights, Lance gave up his phone time with his mom so we could talk. Somehow it also helps Lance come to terms with what he should do and that he has to let me go.

"Jasmine, I heard you got beat up," Penny says with her arms crossed over her chest. She has one leg straight and one slightly bent, making her hip push out to the side. The girls in the bathroom fall silent. Hannah and their friends look at each other, then me. It has been about a month since Lance got beaten up.

Life is back to a kind of normal. The boys are now in outdoor track. It helps the boys with their speed during football season. It's hard work, but they enjoy racing each other and tend not to take it as seriously as football. Hannah loves the last semester of the year. She gets to train with the boys. It is the only time she is in sync with everyone. Her spirits are high. Things are better since Lance got beat up. The fallout from that pulled us together. We are a group again. I have stopped drinking, and talking to Bonny has me back to my happy self again. Penny is trying once again to destroy everything. We have gotten a pattern down that works for us. After track we all go to my house and hang out. Seth and Lance had to give up their jobs until summer. Surprisingly, Susan has been cool about Hannah spending the night. That is making things easier for Hannah and me. On the weekends, Lance, Hannah, Seth, Grant, and Aaron fill Dad in on their speeds and distances at the last meet. Ursula is worse than ever. When Penny told her about Lance fighting, it eliminated any chance of me and Ursula getting along. I argue and fight back most of the time and have been making Ursula's life just as hard as Ursula has made mine. Penny's action has made the others keep her at arm's length. The result is an increase in Penny's criticism of me.

"Shut up. Does it look like she got beat up?" Hannah

jumps in front of Penny, ready to attack her. "What is your major malfunction? Can't you ever give it a break?" Hannah and the rest of the girls have spent the last month fighting Penny's endless attacks. I have forgiven Penny over and over, infuriating Hannah.

"Leave me alone, Penny, or stop coming to my house." I feel panic take over. It is the end of the year. I don't know how she would have known and why it took almost the school year for her to say anything. Maybe it isn't what I think. Looking up, I am relieved that everyone is looking at Hannah and Penny. My face would have surely given the truth away.

"Well, my cousin lives next door to Jasmine." Penny doesn't even blink. "She said she saw Jasmine sitting on her front steps all bruised at the end of the summer."

"Then you're an idiot. Your cousin is full of shit." Hannah is physically shaking. This is the brazen attitude Penny shows day after day. "You are always picking at one of us. One of these days I'm going to lose it."

"Maybe. I was just saying what I heard." Penny turns and leaves with a group of the cheerleaders. They mutter and mumble loud enough for everyone to hear:

"Hannah's always yelling at everyone."

"Yeah, she just was saying what she heard."

"Jasmine just never talks for herself."

"Are you all right?" Hannah askes me.

"Are you?" I laugh, facing Hannah. "You were like a pit bull."

"She's such a bitch! She just starts all the time."

Hannah is still breathing deep. The rest of the girls in the bathroom are still staring at Hannah. All at once, everyone starts laughing. We are all still laughing when we leave the bathroom. I feel bad that I can't tell Hannah the truth. Once again, I am reminded that I am keeping a secret from my friend. Hannah tells the boys the story of what happened in the bathroom and gets mad again.

By the end of the day, rumors have spread about someone beating me up. Everybody is staring at and whispering about me as if I get beaten daily. Hannah is spending her time vehemently correcting whoever will listen. Somehow I make it through the day, and the rumor starts to fade before the last bell, most likely because I have no marks on me. Still, I just want to get home. The stories have brought up an uneasy feeling.

I wait with Hannah for the practice to be over. Hannah's coach has told her to skip a few days of running. I kind of wonder if this is part of why Hannah is so riled up. Hannah doesn't do so well without running. I think back to some of the times Hannah couldn't run in the past. She becomes quite aggressive, I remember, snorting out a laugh. Right before the guys get out, I leave. Lance has some paperwork to do for his mother. Seth keeps asking me about the rumors. I am kind of scared to talk to him, so I just try to not be near him. Today was a lot with Penny's rumors. I just want to go home. I give Hannah a huge hug. Hannah runs off to find Grant.

I walk down the road slowly. I haven't walked home

by myself in some time. It kind of feels good not to have to worry about anyone else. I am thinking about what a bad friend I am. Out of the blue, hands wrap around my shoulder and push me between two buildings. He turns me to face him.

"What the hell are you trying to pull?" He slams my body against the side of the building with each word he spits at me. "I told you to keep it to yourself. You want to ruin everybody's life because you're a whore?" He grabs me by the throat and pulls me close. His breath is cool on my face. "Do you want another one-on-one visit?" He lets me go. "I'm warning you: shut your mouth," he says as he walks off. I slide down the wall, wrap my arms around my knees, and place my head down. I focus on listening to my breath to help me keep it together. All this time there was part of me that thought this was behind me. Almost like he forgot what he did to me. It has been getting easier. I was getting over it, or through it, or just dealing with it. It wasn't supposed to ever come up again. He was never to talk to me. I can't slow my breathing down. I can't catch my breath. What if I die out here?

"Stand up." The voice is cool but firm. I look up and see Seth standing in front of me. I wipe my eyes and scurry up. "I think we need to talk." Seth clutches me by the wrist and drags me behind him. I don't know what this emotion is that I see in him. I don't know if he saw what happened. He hasn't said another word and just keeps dragging me. I am not sure where he is going.

Raindrops start to fall. He keeps moving at the same speed. He pulls me into a Chinese restaurant and has us seated in the very back.

"What was that, Jazz?" Seth asks me. He saw.

"You can never tell anyone." I am ashamed, so ashamed. I can't make eye contact. This is definitely the end of any chance I have with Seth. I just want to crawl under the table. Oh, and if he finds out Seth knows, he may kill Tiffy. I can't have him tell anyone.

"Somehow I need to understand what I just heard because I am trying not to leave this table and go kill him." Seth's words are ice cold. I have never seen him like this. He hates me.

"Seth! Please, no." I grab Seth's hands with my own. Tears come to my eyes. "Please don't tell anyone." I look into his eyes. "Tiffy, he will hurt Tiffy." This is the first time we have touched each other since that day, the day Lance moved in. The day I thought everything was finally going to come together for him and me. But somehow it all fell apart.

"Jazz, start at the beginning, and tell me everything, and I'll decide." Seth's face softened.

We order an appetizer just to be left alone. Once the waiter brings the water, I take a deep breath and start at the beginning, telling Seth about the night *he* showed up at my door. It takes a while to start, then the secret I have kept for seven-plus months comes pouring out of me. I can't stop with the story. At times it is incoherent, but Seth doesn't stop me. I release the burden I have carried. By the end, both Seth and I are crying. Seth says he can't believe I have been dealing with all this by myself and that my behavior this year makes more sense. "Jazzy, there is no way I'm going to let him get away with this. His brother did the same thing, and his father got him off," Seth says to my horror. "We never told Hannah and you. Grant didn't want you to look at him differently."

I explained about the threat to hurt Tiffy and how he had threatened the relationship with my friends, saying they would turn away from me. How I couldn't and can't tell my dad. I am crying because I can finally get it out; I cry because I am not alone; I cry because I thought Seth was never going to talk to me again. I just cry. Seth orders dinner for us both. He moves to sit on the same side as me and holds me. We don't talk much. Once in a while, Seth asks a question to clarify a thought. We stay until closing. Seth walks me home without a word and waits for me to get in the house and lock the door.

He has promised he won't say anything, but he isn't sure he can keep that promise. As Seth walks home, he goes over the whole story again in his head. The vision of Jasmine alone and beaten, and hell—he can't even think it. He punches the wall.

CHAPTER 31

SUNG-GI

"Sung-Gi, please!" Shinan-Hua tries not to show the irritation she feels for what she considers to be my complacency. "You are always doing for everyone with nothing in return, but you won't help your own sister. You are an elder now. Mystic and Julie aren't here, so I couldn't get married now anyway! I want to choose whom I marry." Shinan-Hua picks up a roll that I made for dinner. I bare my teeth and slap her hand. I have tried to listen with an open mind, but my sister is getting on my last nerve.

"I have very little help with the food." My sharp tone and glare have no effect on Shinan-Hua. Shinan-Hua shows no empathy for my frustration; in fact, she is showing contempt. "Why don't you help me?" I slap Shinan-Hua's roll-filled hand again, which is accompanied by a sound from a sharp sucking in of my mouth.

"Have one of the men do it!" Shinan-Hua has no

interest in doing any "domestic" work and finds it degrading because the men don't do it. I am the opposite. I love to cook and bring everyone together. I love meals together and shared time, stories, memories, plans, and games. Having the whole village gather as one huge happy family. Creating the environment to foster inclusion—that is my daily goal and brings me great joy. Not today, though. Shinan-Hua is determined not to marry who she has been paired with.

Shinan-Hua liked training and lives for combat. She wants to be a leader of defense and attack, to train and plan. She doesn't care about cooking and gathering around a fire unless it's to talk fighting styles and stories. Most of all, she doesn't want to get married to a weak, gutless man. The strongest, or second strongest because Ryo is the strongest and best fighter by far, so that she can have the second strongest by her side. She is the best catch, she thinks, and Darton, who she loves, needs to work for her affection. It isn't fair for him to just "get her." I understand her thinking but can't understand why she won't understand what is best for the village.

"OK! OK, what if I can get a competition for your marriage between Darton, Young Sun, and Bancroft? Will you agree to the winner? No matter who?" I have talked to Tybalt and the others about my sister's defiance against traditions. I find it bothersome that the vampires are all for allowing Shinan-Hua to do as she pleases. The group laughs lovingly and will back whatever Ryo and I decide. Ryo won't get involved and will back me also. It is so aggravating that, as a village leader, my sister is the cause of my problems. I also want Shinan-Hua to be next in marriage so she can be second in command. This issue is not making everyone happy, but I make the choice on my sister's behalf.

Ryo and I announce at dinner that Shinan-Hua has agreed to marry the winner of a competition between Young Sun, Darton, and Bancroft. There will be four challenges. The first Perival will come up with. The second Alexandra will do. The third Elsabet will do. The final one will be with Shinan-Hua and will be put together by Tybalt. A large cheer goes up. This is the first time something like this has happened. Tradition has been changed, and competition is on display. Everyone is happy, except the two girls who are now forced to watch their future mates compete for someone else's heart. I have failed them. I promise myself that I will make it up to them. I wish Julie were here with me.

The vampires are pleased and proud of the change. They have learned tradition is important to maintaining order and preserving history and habit. But real growth happens when tradition is respectfully challenged and changed. This young tribe of orphans that they have given their cold hearts to is starting to grow on their own. I hear repeatedly how well I have done. It doesn't feel that way.

"Seriously? This is not fair or right. If it was one of us, Sung-Gi would never have done this," Kate complains loud enough for me to hear. Is she right? I watch out the widow as Kate and Raeleen sit by the water, a small brook that runs behind my new house. I have done this; Kate's and Raeleen's promised men are now in a competition to be Shinan-Hua's mate, leaving the young women in an uncomfortable and embarrassing situation.

Raeleen stays motionless except for her hands that are busy picking at her wolf's fur. She painfully pulls large chunks of fur out of her perfectly still wolf's hind leg. Dana is used to the pain. Raeleen has been doing this since she was young. It breaks my heart. Kate's wolf, Bramwell, gently nudges Kate. He knows Raeleen would soon turn on Kate. Kate has a big heart, and she tries hard, but she is childlike. I don't like what may happen next, and I feel bad. They know I am watching and listening.

Bramwell looks at me; we talked earlier. I talked with all the wolves together. He doesn't like the way Raeleen was pulling Kate out of the group. Bramwell knows that Kate is feeling down. Bramwell can't help but feel disappointed with the possibility that Kate may lose Bancroft. He's been waiting for that. Bancroft is strong and patient, slow to anger, a perfect match, and Bramwell and Hiromi were looking forward to life together. Bancroft loves Kate. Of that Bramwell is sure. We can't figure out why he is pushing to be next to Shinan-Hua as her mate. They get along, but there is no caring beyond respect for the work and devotion each gives to improving their fighting style and the defense of the village. But right now, we decided Bramwell just has to protect Kate from Raeleen.

"I mean, how can we just be pushed out? This is our life. Bancroft said he doesn't want to lose me. But he must do this. I mean, why? Why must he?" Kate has no one to vent to. I know her heart hurts so much. "I don't like the feeling I have toward Shinan-Hua. We were never super close, but we always got along and respected each other. I would go to Shinan-Hua when I had an idea or wanted to improve my fighting technique. Shinan-Hua seemed to be the only one, besides Bancroft and Sung-Gi, who saw the value in my way of fighting. I feel like I lost someone in Shinan-Hua, and now I am uncomfortable with her. I now go out of my way to not be in the same area as her. Even though Bancroft betrayed me, I still feel like it is Shinan-Hua's fault. It feels so lonely."

"Power." Raeleen takes two handfuls of fur and yanks. "The idea of losing Young Sun is more than I can take. I have wanted Young Sun from as far back as I can remember. I have fought to shine in this place. The perfect Sung-Gi and the ultimate fighting machine Shinan-Hua have always outshone everyone. Male, female, vampire, or werewolf, they are the perfect creatures, and everyone dotes on them. Now they team up to take the only thing I care about. To think about all the sacrifices I have made over my life because of the twins and Julie. The trio that thinks they own the world. Now the man I have waited for, Young Sun, who has tried to slip away from me but was promised to me, is able to go to the wonderful twin. When we were matched for life couples, I couldn't believe it. I was so happy and learned all Young Sun's fighting forms so I could be right beside him. The twins just never stop getting their way." Raeleen speaks angrily as she grabs more fur. "Now, on top of everything, Shinan-Hua is going to not take one man but three. Then what? I have to accept the loser of the challenge. The man no one wants? The leftovers? I don't want anyone but Young Sun. I hate the pain in my chest that won't go away." She looks down at the bare skin on her wolf. "Oh my gosh, Dana, I'm so sorry! Are you OK? Just another thing Shinan-Hua has done," Raeleen says with rage. "It doesn't ever stop with those twins and their special rules," she mutters miserably to herself.

That night dinner and the village bonfire were electric with excitement. The vampires were eager to see our little group of humans deal with our first real issue on our own. I still am not sure we did the right thing. I am not sure my idea was the right one. The vampires knew this would and will have long-term effects on the relationships. But this will also make these young ones stronger. We have to learn conflict and to control our emotions. Raeleen and Kate now have to face a new emotion that they have not really had to face before. Ryo and I have the first village issue as elders. Shinan-Hua, Darton, Young Sun, and Bancroft have to pick up the pieces of what they have created in the village. It is the birth of a new day, of new ideas, and of new emotions.

Humans, we are told, give too much to emotions and momentary thoughts. We have short life spans, so it is understandable. Vampires don't care much about the feelings of humans if they can still preform and fight. The rest doesn't matter.

"Tradition keeps community and controls chaos, but questioning and changing tradition is when growth happens," Elsabet says as she looks at her tribe.

CHAPTER 32

JASMINE

Penny is the first to show up at my house the next morning, just as she has most mornings since Lance has moved in. Penny's intensity is driving all of us even further away from her, which is making her more desperate. Her aggression is relentless. She is becoming harder to deal with. Penny's sharp tongue leaves Hannah and me, most days, with hurt feelings. Still, she refuses to be left out and clings to our group as we do what we can to shake her. Even Lance is having less patience with her. I am used to the way she gets. Part of me knows Penny feels left out like I did. I just hope she'll stop thinking of me as the enemy. I am thinking about other things and have little energy for Penny and her attitude today. I try not to let Penny bother me; I feel sorry for her. This morning I am just trying to make it through the morning. I'm kind of klutzy and can't get it together. I guess it is from lack of sleep. I am standing at the top of the stairs with my jacket and backpack all stuck in my hair. I have no idea how this happened. My hair is actually twisted around and through my backpack. I don't know if I should laugh or cry.

Seth is second to come to the house. He walks past Penny, who is standing and waiting for Lance to come down the stairs. Seth and everyone else ignore Penny. It is easier to ignore her than it is to fight with her and listen to her mouth. They say she is the mean one, but I think they are always leaving her out.

"Holy shit. Do you mind?" I am untangling my hair from the zipper in my backpack when Seth grabs me. I am startled. Seth steps behind me and pulls my hair free with skilled hands. He turns my face to his.

"As of this moment you are dating me. OK, Jazz? I didn't want us to start out like this. I won't let on that I know, but this is my one condition. I can keep you safe. He won't dare—" Seth's nostrils flair as he tries to hold his anger down. He looks down at me, and I am looking at him with my eyes wide and eyebrows raised. I am just staring at Seth. Relief flows through me. Last night he walked me home without a word. He told me he would do nothing for now and told me to go in and go to bed. He hadn't even said good night. I have been thinking up to this point that he was never going to talk to me again. My eyes slightly well up, and I bite my lower lip. Seth hugs me, then holds me at arm's length again. "Just come on." Seth puts his arm around my shoulder. "You OK?" he asks as we walk out to the gathering group. "What were you doing to your hair?"

Aaron, Hannah, and Grant have arrived. Lance is walking down the stairs to join everybody. Hannah is happily blocking Penny from coming in the main part of the house. Seth and I come out and join the group with Seth's arm around me. Everyone's mouth drops open, except Penny who beams.

"Jazz has finally agreed to go out with me." Seth holds me close. He looks at Lance and Aaron. "I hope we won't have any problems." Lance stumbles back a little. "I held back, Lance. I can't anymore."

I don't look up; I keep my eyes down at the ground. I am still trying to work through my feelings. I appreciate Lance and all he has done for me. I love Lance, just like I love Hannah. I can't look at him because I feel bad about the joy I feel standing beside Seth.

"What?" Hannah says, then breaks out in smiles. "It's about time." Penny takes the chance to push past Hannah.

"At least you stopped leading Lance on." Penny moves to Lance's side. She slides her arm around his upper arm. He shakes free, turns, and leaves. Grant stares at them. Seth glares back, then smiles a big toothy grin.

"Wait up, Lance." Grant takes off after Lance.

"Happy for you, man. Let's go." Aaron walks out the door. It is a long, quiet walk to school. Seth interlocks his fingers with me, and I walk the whole way watching our hands linked together. I want to savor this feeling. Hannah watches me with glee. She wants me to be happy. Grant is in a bad mood, and Lance doesn't talk to anyone the entire way to school. Penny tries to walk next to Lance, but he quickens his steps when she is near. Seth is deep in thought about how he is going to make it the entire day without killing this asshole. He keeps reminding himself that he promised, but he thinks about how many times I have had to walk with or be in the same room with *him*, and he gets mad again.

When we get to school, Seth walks me to my locker. He stays remarkably close to me. He watches me talk to my friends. "I love how you wrinkle your nose right before you smile, how your face lights up so easily. I've waited for this for a very long time. I am going to enjoy it," he says loudly to himself. I find it hard to focus. I am having outbursts of giggles, and my insides feel like they are lighter than my skin and trying to float out of my body. Everyone is passing us and asking questions. Seth is just staring at me, so I am greeting everyone and answering. When I have organized myself and my locker, Seth takes me by the hand again and leads me to homeroom. The kids stayed in their homerooms for most of the day, getting ready for testing. I don't think there could be anything better. I spend the day sitting between Seth and Hannah, studying. Hannah and I text back and forth even though we are right next to each other. Lance lies his head down and looks out the window during the whole class. Penny sits close to Lance and continues to talk to him even though he is not speaking. Aaron is sitting in front of me. He is chatting as much as Hannah and me. He seems happy about the couple. Strangely, Seth and Grant are quiet. Penny and Lance stay in the classroom during lunch. Penny sets food out for Lance, who silently eats it all, to Penny's pleasant surprise. She breathes a sigh of relief. I can do this, she thinks. When we come back to class after lunch, Lance puts his head back down. By the end of the school day, the entire student body is aware of Seth and my relationship.

I get my homework out after school. I don't know if any of my studying in class has gone to my brain. I'm so happy today. I am thankful for Seth. He told me to wait for him during track. I am happy to have a little time to think. My head has been spinning, and I feel like I've been on a roller coaster with my emotions these last two days. It feels good to have nothing and no one for a moment. Hannah left for the day. She says Grant is going to skip practice and go to her house. She is over-the-moon excited.

When practice is over, Seth and I walk slowly together. Seth opens up to me about how he feels about me and for how long. He tells stories from his perspective from when we were younger. About how he felt when my mother died and Lance lived with me. How he would sit outside my window after Pops thought he had left. How he would follow me home sometimes when I looked sad that first year. How amazing he felt holding my hand the day Lance came back to live with me. How heartbroken he was that Lance was going through so much, which meant he couldn't be happy, and it hurt so much that he just turned his back on me. I tell Seth how hurt and confused I was when he stopped talking to me. Seth points out Lance's point of view. Lance has always been put in charge of my and Hannah's welfare, as well as Bonny's. Seth genuinely believes Lance will be OK if we are happy. Seth talks so candidly about his feelings that I feel shy in a way I have never felt before.

"Are you OK, Jasmine? You have gone quiet." Seth takes my hand. Butterflies hit my stomach. I don't know if I have ever felt this way. "I know you didn't ask for this, but I think it is for the best."

"No, Seth, I like this." I look at the ground and smile to myself. Seth stops, turns me to face him, and kisses me. I feel tingling from the top of my head to my toes. We walk the rest of the way in silence. I focus on the pressure of our hands against each other.

When we get to my house, Seth comes in. I grab two water bottles, and we sit at the table and talk. Aaron texts Seth. He is close enough to catch up with him. Seth jumps up, kisses me, and excuses himself.

Lance is finished filling out the paperwork the landlord wants him to so they can move back in to their apartment in about a month and a half when Bonny gets back. It turns out that the landlord upgraded the whole apartment building and moved people temporarily into Lance's apartment so they could renovate each place. They were going to be able to get their same place, except upgraded. Lance can help the landlord with the work on the apartment during his free time. He is on his way back to Dad's after setting a schedule up. Penny has been waiting the whole time for him. As he goes home, Penny walks beside Lance.

"Are you OK?" She gently takes Lance's arms.

"Penny, go home." Lance shakes his arm free. She puts her hands behind her back and keeps pace with Lance. She thinks of what to say.

"You must have been so shocked when Seth said that this morning. No one seems to be concerned with how you feel," she points out.

"Shut up, Penny, and just please go home." Lance is over the whole thing. He was able to forget and focus on the good for a little while. He is upset, but somehow Penny makes him feel worse. He doesn't hate us. He is just heartbroken. He sees the way I have been looking at Seth lately. I never looked at him like that. He just didn't know if he should keep trying or if by doing that he would lose both of us. He wanted to be alone and think. Every step he has taken today, Penny is there. He knows she must feel the way he does every day; still, he can't help it. Penny is not in his heart. I am. He knows he must stop now.

"Starting in again, honey?" Grant walks up to them.

"Shut up," Penny snaps. She is not going to let anyone get in her way.

"Are you playing with me?" Grant jokes.

"You're such an ass."

"Careful how you speak to me."

"Lance, have him leave me alone." Then she grabs Lance's arm again.

"You think Lance is going to save you? Why would he? No one likes you, honey."

Penny stops walking and turns and faces Grant. She has had enough and won't be bullied anymore. Before she can get her words out, Grant sees Seth and Aaron running at him in full force. Grant realizes what's about to happen from the looks on their faces. Grant pushes Penny out of the way and runs using all his might, fully aware that Seth is faster than he is. As they pass Lance and Penny, Aaron slows down his steps.

"Grant attacked Jasmine." Aaron quickly updates them, then picks up his speed. Like a shot, Lance passes Aaron just as Seth gets his hands on Grant's shoulders.

Hannah slams through my front door. Hannah can feel and hear her heartbeat in her ear. As Hannah breathes in and out, it sounds like a wind tunnel in her head. Aaron comes up, grabbing her upper arm. "Sorry, Hannah, it's bad." He tries to stop her at the door. Hannah sees he has swollen hands and blood splattered on his shirt. Hannah stares in horror, then pushes past him. Time seems to slow down. Hannah feels like she is moving as fast as she can and getting nowhere. Finally, she comes around the corner and sees Lance, Seth, and Grant covered in blood. Grant is on the floor. His face is swollen, cut, and bruised. Hannah steps forward toward him. Grant turns his head away from her. Lance steps in front of her. Blocking her view to Grant with his chest. He puts his hands up.

"You need to see Jasmine." Lance's voice is cool. Hannah doesn't recognize his tone. She has never heard it before. It makes her feel more panic.

"What is going on? Is she in the kitchen?" Hannah moves toward Grant. Seth steps behind Lance to block Grant. The magnitude of the mood overwhelms Hannah. "Grant. He needs to go to the hospital." Hannah is pushing, trying to get around Lance and Seth. The boys stand unmoved.

"He raped Jasmine." Blunt words lash out. "He needs to go to jail." Penny is standing with disdain, watching the whole scene. Her arms are crossed with her perfectly manicured nails showing. "No doctor would help him. He's evil, and we should be calling the police."

"What?" The room stops for a moment. "Shut up." Hannah's face snarls, and she starts for Penny.

"It's true, Han. That's why I called you. This involves you too." Aaron puts his hands on Hannah's shoulders. "You should apologize," he says, looking at Penny. "You don't have to be like that."

"For what?" Penny yells, throwing her hands up in exasperation. She expressed what everyone was thinking. Why were they turning on her? How was this her problem? She is the only levelheaded one here.

"Maybe you should go home, Penny."

Hannah slowly walks past her and goes into the kitchen. Penny follows behind her, glaring back at Aaron.

"No. I'm not leaving. Jasmine is my friend too. I have been part of this whole night."

"Jazzy? Please tell me there's a mistake. Jazzy?" Hannah stands defeated in front of me. I am sobbing in a kitchen chair. I can't bear this situation. I feel so exposed and as if this is all because of me. Strangely, I am comforted by Penny's firm voice defending her. Hannah's voice is barely a whisper. "Jazz?"

"Why should she have to retell it? And to you of all people?" Penny relentlessly spits unfiltered words at Hannah. "You can't tell me you didn't know anything was wrong with your boyfriend or your best friend!"

"Han, I am so, so, so, so sorry, and I felt so bad for not telling you." I start sobbing uncontrollably. My chest hurts so much. I slam my fist against my chest bone to help relieve the emotional pain.

"Why should you be sorry? You didn't do anything wrong. Grant did. What did you do but take more abuse for protecting your friend? She's some friend." Penny stands with her hands on her hips. The whole thing is ridiculous to her. It's clear to her that Grant is wrong and should go to jail. She looks at Lance for some help.

"Shut your mouth before I shut it for you." Hannah is confused and feels like she is slipping into insanity. Penny's voice is like a mosquito buzzing around her head. She can't think with Penny talking. Penny's words are like the little voice in the back of your mind. They are true words that you try to hide from.

"I know this is a lot, Hannah. Penny is right. Jasmine

has nothing to feel bad about." Aaron talks slowly and tells her the whole story. When Aaron's done talking, Hannah continues to stand perfectly still as she has during the whole story. There are tears on her cheeks. She makes no sound as everybody watches her reaction. Lance comes over and holds Hannah. He guides Hannah to Jasmine, and the two girls cry together. Penny watches from a distance. Lance goes and starts to wash his hands in the sink. Aaron follows suit. Grant starts to rise.

"Don't you move," Lance growls. Grant slides back down the wall. "Wait here," Lance says to Seth and Aaron. No one speaks. Lance returns with three large T-shirts. The boys change. Everyone but Grant is gathered in the kitchen.

The house shutters and shakes. Tiffy howls and circles everyone. She seems to grow as she brings the group together. The front door flies open. Hannah, Jasmine, Penny, and Aaron are clumped together in a big, strange hug, half protecting, half hiding. Seth and Lance are side by side, pushed back against the wall. Grant curls into an even tighter ball. Four tall, slender figures walk through the door. Tiffy jumps on the one farther in the back. The once tiny dog has somehow changed into an enormous fluffy dragon of sorts.

"My children, it is time to come home and learn who you are." Susan says as she walks in behind them. "This issue will be taken up later."

CHAPTER 33

SUSAN

Lance, Seth, Aaron, Grant, Jasmine, Hannah, and Penny find themselves standing on the street of a tiny village. In front of them stand the people who they look like. Darton looking at Lance, Ryo at Seth, Bancroft at Aaron, Young Sun at Grant, twins Sung-Gi and Shinan-Hua at Jasmine, Kate at Hannah, and Raeleen at Penny. I am shocked by how they resemble each other. I forgot how they all looked. But moreover, I am glad to be home. So many years away, and the only thing that is missing is my sister, Mystic. Jasmine has the exact face as the twin women in front of her. Hannah has the same face as Kate but is much taller. The other siblings hold similarities also. All fifteen are amazed and confused. The island is howling with a wailing that chills the bones. Sung-Gi, Shinan-Hua, Ryo, Darton, Kate, Young Sun, Bancroft, and Raeleen have never heard this sound. They tense and instinctively encircle the new members.

"These are your siblings. The babies who survived," Elsabet says over the sound. "The ones you thought were dead. We had to keep them safe until they came of age. They are your siblings, but they also have the blood of fairies. They are highly prized in the vampire world. They are the reason for the attacks. We must train them quickly and find their unique traits."

I watch Jasmine as Elsabet speaks. She looks like something inside is starting to break. Without control, she throws her head back and screams back at the voices before she collapses. "The fairies have felt your presence here. They are the ones that saved you. They are the ones that placed you with your parents, making them promise to protect you. You are a part of them and them a part of you. One is a father to you all, in a way."

Jasmine's whisper remembers this place, remembers the connection to the direct line of fairy blood. She wakes to a huge number of tiny, strange creatures, like little children. They are cradling the new kids and stroking their hair with little but strong hands. Penny is sitting with two little children, and they are making flowers bloom. Seth, Hannah, Aaron, and Lance are being inspected by at least ten of these little not children, fairies Grant is nose to nose with a floating, flying boy. The only boy. The other adults they just met, siblings, are in a circle, watching them. "Jasmine? Are you OK?" Sung-Gi asks. Jasmine looks between her and Shinan-Hua. "My gosh, this must be a lot for you all."

"Yes, a lot for them."

"But look how cute they are."

"And soft."

"Our babies are back."

"Sung-Gi, you take care of our special babies that are back." On and on the group of close to a hundred fairies chats and touches the seven kids who finally came home.

The next few hours, our fifteen shocked young adults talk and put the pieces together. The stories of real live vampires, fairies, werewolves, and the rest, not to mention Tiffy. No one seems to know what Tiffy is. The little fairies are bouncing around with each other and the humans. I see Jasmine and the others are getting tired and ready to get some questions answered before they go to bed. The fairies quietly retreat as if reading the kids' minds. I retreat also and let the humans have some time alone.

CHAPTER 34

JASMINE

This is like the strangest dream that you can't wake up from. I can still feel the little fairies touching me even though they are no longer here. Not to mention that I have twin older sisters. All of us have siblings. What in the actual hell is going on? Did Dad know? Where is Dad? Will I never see him again?

We have a long conversation of which most is not registering in my mind. I think they are explaining what is happening. Something about us going to bed, but they have to train. Train for what? I want to ask. But my mind isn't clear, and I am so tired.

None of us can keep sleep at bay. We are shown to a large cabin. Grant asks to stay with Young Sun to the relief of the rest of us. When we are alone, we give hugs to each other, even Penny, and go to sleep. I have just a brief moment to kiss Seth.

We sleep that night and the whole next day.

The next evening the seven of us are called to the vampires' village underground. We are shown around the city. It is magnificent, a combination of a ruined, ancient cave community and a high-tech city. Clothing stores with vampires making the clothes from cotton. I mean, spinning the tread. Unbelievable. A wine maker next to other kinds of alcohol, blood drinks, milk drinks, and everything in between. Coffee shops with pastries, sandwich shops, jewelry shops, beauty salons, barber shops, bookstores, tons of eateries. Plumbing, electrical, theater, blood-making labs, and anything else one could think of. So amazing. We just watched, listened, and learned with our mouths open and eyes wide. Alexandra pulls us into an abandoned café.

CHAPTER 35

SUSAN

"You young ones have had some challenges!" Alexandra hates emotional things. I try not to smile as she goes through her talk. I have missed this Amazonian queen. I am standing behind her as a liaison of sorts until these kids get acclimated. Alexandra never liked emotions, even when she was human. Now it just seems ridiculous to all of us from our endless life perspective. Such short lives. Always focusing on what dreadful things happen to the poor little humans. Alexandra will not let these problems corrupt this village. "I know you feel the world has been unkind to you." Penny nods in agreement. Jasmine looks up slightly. Grant looks down. Tybalt walks in at this moment. "You need to get over your problems and leave them in this room right now." Alexandra's voice is flat. I almost laugh. I have been in the human world too long. I feel full of emotion. Tybalt looks at me. I crinkle my eyebrow and laugh at his expression. He rolls his eyes, winks, and turns to face the kids. He speaks.

"What our fearless warrior is trying to say is that life here depends on following a way of life. Aggression and violence are only in fighting. You will partner with who we tell you to and forgive everything that has happened before now. If you ever attack anyone who is not your enemy, I will eat you up, Grant." With that Tybalt flashes his fangs, which grow out fast, cutting his lip and causing bleeding. His vampire face in horrifyingly full view for all of them to see. His eyes turn blood red. His face becomes translucent. The veins on his face become dark purple and shine through the skin. "Now talk it out."

We start the conversation, and the group talks for a long time, yelling, crying, and coming to terms with all of this. After several hours, the rest of the village comes looking for them. Jasmine stands and then walks over to Grant and gives him a hug. "I forgive you." Jasmine has heard and understands it all. I see she is done with talking about this and is exhausted both mentally and physically. She walks out to see her sisters.

Lance comes forward and puts his hand on Grant's shoulder. "If Jazzy can, then I have too also." The rest of the group walk out without talking to Grant. I don't think Seth has let it go.

In the street of this underground city, music starts playing. "One night off. That is it!" Alexandra feels like the whole village is losing it. I put my hand on her shoulder. "Has everyone lost their minds?" She looks up at me.

Music fills the night air. As I walk Alexandra in, I smile at the scene. Aaron finds the vampire who is playing the music finally. "May I?" He connects his phone and plays "Party in the USA." The vampire nods in agreement. Jasmine and Hannah yell and start really dancing. The rest of their childhood friends join in. The rest of the humans from the village try to copy the movements. Everyone is singing, dancing, and laughing. It is a sight to see. We have family members from many countries and many backgrounds. Some have chosen not to change. The exotic beauty that dances on this ground cannot be imagined by any human. Women who read oracles from before the world of religions now dance as if the gods are speaking to them. Previous kings and queens from all over, ladies of the night, warriors from every country, and era. Moving and gyrating as one big mass.

CHAPTER 36

MOTHER

Francis swings open the oversized double door of the mansion's main sitting room by thrusting both hands against them. His voice echoes with forced exuberance in the great room, shaking even the air. "Aww, my love, how exquisite you look today." Francis holds his arms out in an exaggerated grand gesture. A wide smile spreads across his face. His cape breathes in and out with each step. Francis's eyes are fixed on me, his love, his maker, his queen. I am the last of the most ancient vampires. I sit on a thrown-type chair that my beautiful Darius made for me. I am stroking a boy's hair. The boy is about thirteen, thin, and naked. Lots of naked bodies are lying around my feet and around the room. Francis's voice is starting to stir the sleeping bodies.

"Home at last, my darling." My words seem to linger in the air for a moment when I speak. Almost as if each word is slower than the moving lips. I am the only vampire who can do this. The only one who can control air and sound. There are other beings that can do it, but they don't utilize the gifts given to them. Mystic and Susan just plain wouldn't dare. "My pets, you may leave me now." The human bodies that are carelessly spread everywhere get up on hands and knees as they move on all fours. They soundlessly transform into wolves and leave as a pack. The puppies are the last to leave. The smallest one is the one that I was petting. He looks back, but he no longer matters to me except for food. I am a bit peckish. My touch has an energizing property for attracting living creatures to me. My mind and body have been alive since history began. That transcends through me. I have many whispers and shadows attached to me. The puppy turns its head back to the pack and rushes to catch up.

A whisper is, to a human, the attachment from the divine realm. It is part of the human soul and person. It is also part of a collective. Humans have no idea how to use the gifts given to them. Shadows are the same thing but connected to the earth. When I kill or turn, I take on their shadow or whisper. I am invincible.

As the pack walks out, Francis reaches my chair. He leans over and kisses me, his ancient creature.

"Where is our Darius?" I smile at my husband. I have loved Francis for over fifteen hundred years. But I have loved lots of things for lots of years. Things and companions come and go, no matter how long our time together. For now, I am joyful and like the playfulness of my latest husband. I laugh at Francis's gestures. I know my face and voice light up when I laugh. Best way to catch an enemy. "Does he not come to see me?" I lift my left hand to brush away a fallen strand of hair from Francis's face.

"Why, Mother, of course I run first to you." Darius strides into the room, arms lifted. Julie is directly behind him. I can sense Julie trying to be as small as she can. I know their thoughts; she hopes not to be noticed. Renton is beside Julie in wolf form. How I hate those purebred wolves. So much larger than mine.

Darius is my heart too. I can't stand him with that human. I can smell and feel the disgraceful family that dejected us. After all I did for them. I made them. I protected them for years. No loyalty. No thankfulness. I am to be worshiped. This smelly little girl is lucky I am so in control. In the days gone by, villagers would have made her a sacrifice. Her bloodline goes way back. I have sheltered her ancestors, and she doesn't greet me on her knees. Darius's obsession with this family line, this lineage that once was my oracles, witches, and handmaidens. Because of my love for my women from the past, I have blessed this line with my protection. But the last few generations are trying my will. If I weren't the real goddess that I am, I would have killed them all. When the women that I love are reincarnated in useless lumps of human flesh made for my nourishment, it does sadden me. Julie, Shinan-Hua, Sung-Gi, and Nina are part of my cherished love Ruth's descendants. Sung-Gi is the reincarnated child

Ruth had and I raised. Her whisper remembers me and all I have done for her. I will never hurt her because her soul is my child. Shinan-Hua is the reincarnation of my strongest, most-favored bodyguard who reincarnated many times as my defender. Now she is my enemy. I will not hurt her. Now I have two of the descendants in front of me. Lumps of useless flesh, even compared to their family and ancestors. I don't want to see any more decline in the lineage. I should wipe these two out. If I take their whisper, they can't reincarnate. Julie and Nina, what to do? Nina can't reincarnate, so there ends one problem.

Julie—so weak that she wishes she could wrap her arms around her dog's neck and feel his fur against her. I am the one who she should be clinging to. Not that mutt and not my sweet Darius. Renton is here in front of me in wolf form because a wolf is an even match with a vampire. Not me. There isn't a wolf who would rise against me. But why don't I have wolves like this? My wolves are on that island. The evil Elsabet and the rest have taken my strong wolves and left me to create new small, weaker wolves. When wolves are made, they are smaller. My wolves that Elsabet took did not believe in changing humans, so the pups they have are bigger and bigger. Mystic, my loving daughter, keeps pace behind the problem Julie—to protect Julie but also because she loves and misses me. Whatever happens or whatever they say, all vampires are drawn to me. Most are too scared to get close, but they want to. Every living creature wants to, even to the death.

Mystic—she knows where she wants to be. I am her comfort. Behind Mystic are Darius's wives: Nina, Tarissa, and Melissa. The cowardice's vampires stay way behind Mystic. These are newer vampires made by Darius. Darius made them at separate times to upset me when I didn't give him his way. It worked, all but Melissa. I like her. But I see them as a sign of defiance from one of my favorite children. They know if they were ever to bring attention to themselves, I would kill them. Well, I can't kill Nina, and I don't want to kill Melissa. If I kill Tarissa, it will do no good. She is a good soldier. But they are also required to greet me and should on their knees. Mystic outpaces Julie and reaches me before Julie does. She sits at my feet and rests her cheek on my knee.

I smile at the weak Julie. "Is it that time already?" My smile is easy. My eyes twinkle. One would think I was happy to see Julie. No one knows what is on my mind. I never give away anything.

"Yes, Mother. You look so beautiful as always," Julie says as she and Renton approach. Renton keeps his head low. I see him look at the others in the wolf pack. He cares little about them. They are half his size from transforming so often. I know he is the smallest of the wolves because he comes here for six months every year. He hates this moment, but it determines how the six months will go. He takes whatever I give. He has been thrown through the room on many occasions. Julie steps up Renton next to her.

"Go away, you mutt." I spit at and kick Renton with

enough force to shake him, not kill him. He hits the far wall and collapses. He tries to stand and reassure Julie. Mystic moves quickly to his side. She doesn't look at me. It makes me want to rip him apart and see if she can fix that. Mystic's hands go over and through his body, and the pain dissipates. Mystic doesn't speak to me. I am not to be corrected, but she wants to; I can feel it. Julie freezes. She knows she can't check on Renton. Julie takes a deep breath and continues talking to me. I now have a snarl on my face because of this group of ragtag misfits making me unhappy.

"May I kiss you, Mother?" Julie smiles, pushing other thoughts from her mind.

"Yes, my child." Julie leans down. I know she has a challenging time. I have no scent. It is so strange, Julie explained before to the twins. Dead air. No air. Julie kisses me on the cheek. To her, my skin is cold and clammy. Soft but always kind of damp. Julie stands up and backs away slowly. "I think your manners are getting better. Your thoughts, at least."

The three of Darius's wives step up to give their greetings to me. Julie goes back behind Darius, and Renton moves to her side, limping slightly. Mystic moves back to my feet. Her energy calms me. In a minute or two, I feel better.

CHAPTER 37

JASMINE

Penny, Hannah, and I wake up at noon the next day. We talk about the night and the new world we are in. None of us talk about the world we left behind. I try not to think about Dad. Sung-Gi comes in.

"Let us all get ready for the day. We have a lot of training to do." Sung-Gi smiles. "But first, we eat." With that, she spins on her heels. The three of us follow her. We are so hungry. The meal is outside on the largest table any of us newcomers have ever seen. Humans are around the table talking. Most we have seen before. Sung-Gi leads them to the center of the table. Lance, Seth, Aaron, and Grant are already sitting. Questions on all sides flow. Everyone wants to know how the other lives. Everyone is talking at once, laughing and telling stories. After the meal, the men go off along with Shinan-Hua. The rest of the humans clear the table and clean the dishes. Hannah, Penny, and I are amazed that doing dishes entails taking them to a small river and washing with no soap in the river, then lugging the dishes up to the table that is now clean and laying them out to dry. So much work just to eat.

"What do you do when it rains?" Penny asks.

"Most of the time we eat in smaller groups. Only once or twice a week do we eat together," Raeleen says.

The group moves to join the rest of the men who are already training. Bancroft and Ryo are collaborating with Lance, Seth, Aaron, and Grant. We girls are put into painful stretching positions. Training goes on until dusk, when we break for food.

"Thank goodness," Penny says. We are sore and tired from so much work. After we eat, we get up to go to bed.

"Are you ready?" Alexandra walks up to us. "I will be working with you tonight." A groan escapes the group. "Enough! We do not respond to anything like that." The force of her words shuts the sound down. We all stand a little bit straighter.

The whole group trains. Lance, Seth, Aaron, and Grant work on moves with small knives. Hannah, Penny, and I learn the bow and arrow. Finally, at about one in the morning, Elsabet joins us with seven wolves.

"These are your wolves," Elsabet says as a wolf stands in front of each of us. "Tomorrow you will go on a three-day trip with your wolf and learn all about one another. Your wolves are part of you. They protect you and support you. You need to have a mutual understanding and respect for each other. Most wolves know or have heard about their humans at an early age. You seven have to start from nothing. Get some sleep. Wolves wake up at around five. Wolves, please say hello in human form." The wolves change. Hannah and I just stare in wonder at the beautiful creatures before us. I bow, not sure what the greeting should be. Hannah half bows.

"You are naked! You all are naked," says Penny in surprise.

"Well, I don't wear clothes when I am a wolf, so I don't when I am in person form." Penny's wolf smiles.

"I...I...I was just caught off guard," Penny stutters shyly.

Lance, Seth, and Aaron have handsome dark-haired men. Grant hasn't heard any of what has been going on. He is looking at the most beautiful being that has ever walked the face of the earth as far as he is concerned. Hannah glances over and feels a slight jab of jealousy. She was unaware she still would feel anything for him. Our wolves look similar, like Grant's, but the eyes are darker. Grant's wolf has hazel-blue eyes. The group talks briefly. The exhaustion reclaims us, the young humans. We all go to sleep without another word. Not even a "good night" to each other.

The next day the seven of us get out of bed. Each one of us is sore, a pain we have never felt, and tired but excited for the day. I am a little afraid I will not remember which wolf is mine. I don't want to hurt my wolf's feelings. Gyda is my wolf's name. As I come out to where they are all sitting, I see Gyda right away. I run to her and hug her, running my fingers through her furry coat. A bit shocked at my own action, I am pleased to see the others have similar responses, and, even better, Gyda nuzzles against me.

The older villagers and their wolves encircle us. Everyone is happy for us. Shinan-Hua gives each a bag. "Here is food and a small amount of water. There are streams everywhere, so don't worry." As she comes to me, she passes her bow and arrow. "Practice while you are out there. Always practice." She gives the command to the whole group. Shinan-Hua continues. "You have blindfolds. After you have spent today with the blindfolds on, please put them on and keep them on for the rest of your time together. You will spend the first part of your day with just your wolf. As the sun sets, you will join as a group, so your wolves can hunt and eat. The rest of the time you all will be together."

Bancroft steps forward. "Your relationship with each other is especially important, and as a group, you must bond in a way that means you can depend, without a doubt, on each other and your group's wolves. You all are a pack within this pack."

Raeleen takes her turn to talk. "The first part of your walk, you will be in person form. This is so you can speak with each other and get used to being naked." Raeleen smiles and winks at Penny.

The small tribe is given a few more instructions. Each human leaves with a little pack of food, a small canister of water, sticks that you drag on a box to light—matches, they called them—a bow and arrow, and a spear. Gyda slides up to me and nudges her head under my arm. I rest my arm on Gyda's back and put my fingers into the warm fur.

We are about an hour into the walk. It is painful since shoes are not allowed. The group separates, and the wolves transform into people form. Gyda and I talk, easily changing from one subject to another. We talk about the history of this land, what my world was like, Dad, and how much it hurts not to be near him. Some talks lead to tears, and some lead to laughter. The day goes fast, and the small tribe meets up again. No one can miss the large scratches on Grant's face and chest or the teeth marks on the back of his neck. Hannah and I look down. Penny grunts loudly and rolls her eyes. The guys do not react at all. No one speaks of it. Grant has his head down. The wolves blindfold us.

"Listen and learn the sounds around you. Hearing, smelling, and feeling are as important as sight." I know it is Grant's wolf that speaks to us. She must be the leader. "Figure out where we are by our calls. You each have a part of you. One is called a whisper. Your whisper is part of you and part of the heavens. Whispers help you communicate with each other and with us. The other is your shadow. Shadows help you communicate with the earth. It is the same as your whisper, but they help with your needs. Shadows can be selfish. Not because of bad intentions, just because they know what you need. Get in touch with your whisper and shadow."

With that, they leave us and take off to eat. We sit with our backs together, listen to the howls, and try to pick our wolf. We try to smell, but it feels weird for all of us, and each time we try, we end up laughing. We try to feel our whispers and shadows. I can't quite understand; part of me does, but part of me doesn't. I am trying to figure out what that means. Suddenly we hear a bone-chilling howl. Soon another, and another. The world explodes in eerie wails. Hannah and I grab for each other and hold hands.

"Don't worry. They will not let anything happen to us." Grant surprises us with his calm words. I take a deep breath and let go of Hannah's hand. I listen. I try to find Gyda's sound. The cries change to quick bark-like sounds, kind of like a chirp from a bird. It is hard to explain the sound, I think. The sounds are far off and not all together. They are moving at a fast pace. They are signaling to each other. I am proud I figured it out. There's a loud and awful cry of another kind, followed by all the wolves howling in unison.

"They have killed something." Penny points out what everyone else has figured out.

We listen as the wolves eat, clean themselves, and play with the fairies who came and found them. Figuring the fairies out took some time. They listen to the creatures of the night: frogs, tons of insects, flies, and mosquitoes. Occasionally, a fairy would tickle them one by one. The smell of the fairies gave them away, like a field of flowers and herbs. Plus, they giggled the whole time.

The wolves came back. They have a strong smell—earth mixed with wet dog. It was not bad, but not as nice as the fairies' smell. Gyda comes up and nudges me. I stand and put my arm on Gyda's back. Raindrops hit my face. Our troop wanders throughout the island for the next two days without seeing and without the wolves changing into person form. We still have to practice the fighting forms and the bow and arrow. It takes a lot of time to figure out how to do this. Our wolves guide us. I start to be able to communicate with Gyda and the others without words. We practice group meditation for about five minutes every morning and night. Fairies make it hard to concentrate.

We return bloody from falling, thorn bushes, running into limbs, slipping in the mud, and other missteps. We are hungry, sore, and tired from no sleep, but we have done what the mission required and are a tight pack. We jump happily in the river with the wolves and wash off. Getting out of the water, we are ready for sleep. Alexandra is standing at the edge of the camp. "Time to train. You have missed three days. You have to make up for it." Her face softens. "But first, there are some people for you to see." She leads us to a big house. I don't remember it looking so modern. Standing on the front step is Dad.

"*Dad!*" I run.

"*Pops!*" The rest are right behind me. I reach him first and jump into his arms. I get squished by the rest hugging him.

"And me?" Bonny is standing in the door. We run to her. "Come eat." Bonny pushes us in through the door. She looks different. She has gained a little weight.

We shovel food into our face as Dad and Bonny explain that they were given a choice to come live here. They got here the day we left with our wolves. They each have a wolf. Bonny's wolf has been taking her out to run and walk every day. She has a few fairies that come to visit her every day. She says she enjoys them so much. Dad's wolf and the rest of the villagers helped him "whip" the house into shape. It is the biggest house, and we are all going to live here. Well, sleep here.

CHAPTER 38

JULIE

Finally, Darius, Renton, Melissa, Tarissa, Nina, and I leave the awful visit. I am thankful that Renton and I are still alive. It feels wonderful to have survived. We all go back to my place. Each wife, including me, has our own place and an understanding to respect each other. It is no secret that Nina gets jealous from time to time but knows she can never show it when it comes to me. I am Nina's niece from before she was turned. She still has affection for me and her now dead sister, my mom. We wives have bonded. As they lounge on my couch, they watch me eat a large bowl of ramen noodles cross-legged on the floor. There were times when they forgot to feed me. So Darius has a special chef who is always on call to feed me. I like the chef. She leaves out a snack for later tonight. The bowl of ramen is perfect. Renton is in the other room eating too. I don't think about what he is eating. It could be the remains of a body that he drank from. He never tells me. Once, long ago, I walked in on him eating what looked like a human leg. He can't complain about it. I don't think he minds. Ugh, I just don't like thinking about it.

"I need to eat too, Darius," Tarissa says.

"You should have come to work," Melissa answers as she tilts her head and looks at her sister wife with a smirk. "But we could go out." She winks at me. I love going out to the clubs with them.

"Oh, yes, *please!*" I spray food while I speak, getting excited. The others laugh.

"Well, I guess that decides it." Darius grins at the four of us. His expression gives me goose bumps. It is sexy, dangerous, and loving. My sisters, that's what I call them, yell out in delight. Renton comes in. Melissa fills him in on our plans.

There are regular humans who love to be fed off of. The club we choose is the safest place for me. I run to the closet. Darius always fills it with the newest styles for me. They are nothing like what I wear on the island. These clothes are sexy and flashy. Darius lies across the bed, laughing and commenting on the different outfits. My sisters are pulling different outfits they want to see on me. Getting dressed is as much fun as going out. The energy is high. More vampires meet us in the lobby as we head out. I always find it amazing how they all move together without words. Renton stands in the back in human form. He doesn't seem as though he enjoys all of this, but I think he really does. All the female vampires watch him. He is extraordinarily handsome in human form. Melissa slides her arm through his. They have always had a good relationship. Darius doesn't care. It keeps the flea bag away from my side, he says. My feelings are mixed. I love both of them, but I am Renton's human, and their relationship makes me feel as though I'm in second place. I know it's silly and always try to encourage them, but the day after they are together it is always a little weird between Renton and me. None of that matters tonight, though. I want Renton to have as much fun as he can. It was a painful day for him, and Melissa can help him forget better than I can.

"Darius, my man!" The doorman at the club grabs Darius's hand and pulls him close, patting him on the back with his free hand as a way of greeting. Darius winks at me. He finds these changes to the basic handshake funny.

"What's up, Johnny?" Darius smiles at his new vampire. He's just years old. Johnny bows slightly to Melissa. He tried not to eye Renton too much. No one had ever seemed close to Melissa like this. Not even Darius. Melissa kisses him on the cheek. She is his pack leader. She is not part of a "family." A family has one hundred or more, and a pack has one hundred or less. Darius keeps the pack safe. With the power of Darius and his family, Melissa's pack will remain untouched and unbothered by other vampires without a declaration of war. Unlike Nina or Tarissa, Melissa is not and never was in love with Darius. She loves her pack and being a leader. She is Darius's wife solely for the status and protection of her pack. Darius is aware of Melissa's motives—all of us are—but loves her spirit and brain for business. The relationship works for both.

Darius is working to run the family someday, so he can bring down Elsabet and the others once and for all. To do this he needs more vampires aligned with him. Mother and Francis will never let him gain control because they know he will go after Elsabet. They want the old ways to come back, when they were gods. They are against turning too many to vampires. To be a vampire was a special privilege given only after much thought. Francis is worried about Darius and how he turns humans without telling him or Mother. Darius knows he will have the upper hand very soon. He says I will be his full time and Elsabet will join his wives or be destroyed.

Elsabet was the one and only thing Darius wanted. As a human, Darius was mesmerized by Elsabet. Thankfully, Mother fell for Elsabet's father, Francis. Francis's only condition was that his daughter would be turned also. Since 800 AD, Darius and Elsabet were together. They loved each other, were devoted to each other. For a thousand years. Then, overnight, Elsabet ripped out his heart and destroyed the whole family. As she lives as a goddess in her little world, he is living as an undesirable thug. He had almost destroyed them all once before. Now he would bide his time and finish what he started sixteen years ago. He also will get those seven special humans. He has asked me if new humans have come home. I have no idea what his plan is, but he is obsessing about them. I have never heard anyone talk about it. I don't think we have what he is looking for. Who cares tonight?

Melissa makes her pack work. Most for one of her businesses, but a few she sends out to do human jobs so she can keep an eye on the human world and its changes. She never wants to be irrelevant and has plans of her own to become one of the most powerful vampires to have ever lived. But, for now, she is happy doing what she is doing. Her guilty pleasure is Renton. If she has a weakness, he is it.

Johnny lets them into the bass-pumping, light-flashing, body-seating club. This club is known for its vampire groupies. The humans who want to be vampires. The humans who get an adrenaline rush from being in a club frequented by vampires and seedy characters. The different forms of vampire worshipers that find the atmosphere to their liking. But in this city, humans are everywhere, so most of the club's population is regular humans who know this place is always a fun time. The vampires don't try to stand out. The frenzy of dancing and smelling human sweat and the energy can make for a frantic, scary night for the regular person just trying to have fun. The club has the highest number of unsolved deaths.

Tonight no one has cause to worry. All vampires are on their best behavior when I am in town. I stay close to Darius. He keeps one hand on the small of my back as we make our way through the crowd. I keep both hands on my clutch in front of me and my eyes straight ahead to the table I know is ours. I don't want to bring attention to myself. It wouldn't be hard; I am sandwiched between Darius and Nina. I have Tarissa, Melissa, and Renton behind me. The group of us, the beauty of our group, stops most all creatures, vampire and human. I have grown so much. I look like Nina's twin. My body is more muscular from all the training I do. I keep my hair back when I am with Elsabet, so it is very long, curly, shiny, and healthy with light-brown highlights at the temples. Nina's hair falls in large loose curls to the bottom of her shoulder blades. Nina's body is curvy. It is hard not to stare at her figure. As the river of Darius's group flowed into the ocean of the club, the atmosphere seems to energize itself. The night commences with dancing and laughter. I think this is the best time I have ever had in my life as my body rises and falls to the heavy beat of the music. I look at my sisters who are all bouncing in rhythm. I smile as I turn around to see the whole place is dancing like one beating pulse. Hair flying, body parts shaking, sweat spraying, the liveliness of every ounce of space in the club can be felt by every sense I have. It's intoxicating. I look at Darius who is dancing with me. It feels like magic to be having this much fun, to be this free.

CHAPTER 39

SUNG-GI

Our village has changed so much in such a short time. Julie will be so surprised when she gets back home. Love and laughter have joined us, along with the new people of our village. Pops, as we all call him, gets the forgotten of our village engaged with us every day. I never realized we left them out. We all were eating together, but he and Bonny have given them all new purpose. Our village is bustling with a new and different energy. I don't make meals anymore. The other villagers do. They tell stories we have never heard before.

Pops and Bonny give hugs, give pats on our back, and tell us we are doing a good job. It is so queer to have these warm, fuzzy feelings. They have married couples off. Penny, Hannah, and my sister worked with the vampires to make fancy white dresses for the weddings.

My beautiful sister Jasmine is almost like a fairy. She hugs all of us a lot. Shinan-Hua took a long time to get used to the affection. I think if Jasmine wasn't our sister, she would have thrown her. Jasmine isn't as strong physically as the others, but her inner love binds us all.

Jasmine is so in love with Seth. They are wonderful to watch. Penny and Lance are now a couple. Grant and Hannah work hard together. Neither one is interested in relationships, but they work hard on fighting skills. Grant, at first, had a very hard time. But with all of us working with him, he learned to balance his shadow. His shadow was dominating his thoughts and feelings. He has worked the hardest. He took Jasmine and Hannah, along with all their wolves, out for two days. I don't know what happened, but he is different. He is one of the strongest leaders and gives Ryo advice sometimes.

It turns out these kids don't have fairy blood. What happened is Darius told the male fairy about sex. The little fairy pushed the sexual nature and the seed and egg of the female. So they have some magic protecting them, but no blood.

Tiffy is the strangest creature we all have ever seen, an ancient creature that looks like a cross between a dragon and a shaggy dog. He follows Pops everywhere.

Bonny is like a mother to all of us. I go to her just to talk about my thoughts. I can say anything I want, and she listens. It is wonderful.

Alexandra has had the hardest time with all of this. She raged when Pops said we need a day off to celebrate life. They agreed one day a month was just to celebrate everything. We dance like crazy all day long. Creatures from the deeper part of the island have started to join us. An old gnome who watches the babies of different kinds comes up with them once a week in the daytime to talk with Bonny. We all love those days, playing with all the young ones.

This island has become a wonderful place.

CHAPTER 40

JULIE

It is the last week for Mystic and me. I don't want to go. I don't want to lose even a second with Darius, but this morning I just am not able to move. A wave of nausea washes over me. I lean over the bed unable to move. My head feels like it is splitting open as I vomit uncontrollably onto the floor. Darius wakes, and Renton breaks the door down. His teeth are in full werewolf mode. Darius hisses and grows his teeth out. The two circle each other.

"Stop," I whisper. Both run to my side. "I think I have food poisoning. I feel so sick." I lean over to vomit again. Renton and Darius look at each other in fear of what could be wrong. Renton snaps into person form. "I will call Mystic."

"Call Mystic," Darius says at the same time.

Mystic confirms that I am pregnant, that I am having a fairy and an immensely powerful one at that. Quickly they all pack me up. Mother will never allow this baby to be born if she can stop it. We tell no one. The vampires who watch over us are dismissed. Humans are hired to drive twenty cars in different directions. Mystic puts an essence of my whisper plus a potion that mimics me in each car to prevent any chance of searching for me. She takes a car on her own. Renton takes a car on his own. Darius carries me on his back, cloaking our scent.

He runs for nights with me clinging on. We stop during the day at unusual places with people he does business with who Mother and the rest don't know. He starts as the sun is setting and goes until the sun is too much for him. Being on his back, shaken around, does not help me at all. I just want to die. It takes a week for us to get back. Darius is careful not to take a path that would have a vampire searching for us.

Renton makes it back first. He fills the others in. When Darius arrives with me, there is a boat waiting filled with werewolves. Darius and I get on the boat. We hit land in the middle of the day. Darius is in pain from the sun. I am still so sick I can't help him. The wolves don't care to help him. They would prefer he die.

The wolves get out of the boat. The whole village is there except the vampires. Sung-Gi and Shinan-Hua walk to me and take me from Darius. A new group of teenagers I have never seen is standing at the edge of the group. A large barrel of a man picks me up. I have never seen him either. A strange woman comes over with a damp cool cloth. What the hell is going on? I know they are friendly. But who are they, and why are they in my home?

They have heard about me, of course, but they have never met me, and I haven't met them.

They look on at the vampire who killed their family. All the wolves sing at me. Renton noses me in this new man's soft arms.

"Where are you taking her?" Darius breaks through the sound. He steps toward me. Four fairies gently lead me away in this man's arms.

CHAPTER 41

JASMINE

We look on the scene quietly. It is weird after six months that something new is happening. The group of us looks vastly different. We are leaner, stronger, faster, and in tune with ourselves. A different kind of confidence exudes from us. Grant is a humble, fair leader. We watch with the rest of the village as one fairy walks up to Darius. She looks with her child face at Darius as his fangs show through. He doesn't look like he is going to attack her. He looks scared. The fairy tilts her head, never breaking eye contact. As she tilts her head back the other way, her looks melt away; she becomes something grotesque. Hissing, she opens her mouth and double rows of teeth emerge. Wings cut through her skin on her back. Her skin, as well as her eyes, turns bright red. Her pupils change to a blue violet. Her jawline grows until her chin is midchest. Her mouth is wide enough to bite a head clear off. The hiss has changed to a screech. The sound of it is enough to put fear back into Darius's cold heart, along with all of us who are watching the scene play out. She is still staring at Darius, tilting her head from side to side. Only now she is hovering above the ground, eye level with Darius. Darius can feel the breeze from the wings and the soft smell of jasmine, lavender, and heather. He can't turn his head; he is frozen. In all his vampire life, he had never known fear like this. Now he smells the blood from the fairy's protruding teeth. It was the most enticing smell he has ever smelled, and at the same time, it is the scariest smell. Darius thinks this is the end. He will never see Julie or his child.

"No touching her!" The previously simple-minded, beautiful creature mumbles through overgrown vampire teeth. The blood from the teeth ripping her gums splatters on Darius's face. "Do you think to kill that which we love?" the voice snarls. "Do you think to harm us or those we protect?" Blood and spit fly at Darius from the purest killing machine the heavens could create. The most peaceful and most violent creature. The true alpha and omega. All of us are frozen.

Darius drops to his knees and bows his head in defeat. "Julie is having a fairy," he whispers. A heaviness not felt for a thousand years fills his chest. "I am the mate to her. I would never hurt her. I love her." Loss, sorrow, and pain bear down on him. Human emotion once forgotten pulses through him. Tears stream down his face. Bloody tears.

The fairy lands back on the ground and stands still. All Darius can see is her feet. He feels her small hand on his chin. As she lifts it to look at his face, his eyes meet the child again, barely dressed because much of the clothing tore during her transformation. Her small face, with small blood droplets, looks at Darius as she had before. We are all still frozen.

"Stay away for now." The big brown eyes look down at Darius. "Trouble is coming. Protect what we love. Protect and you will see Julie." She turns and walks in the direction the others took Julie. Darius has no intention of going any farther. We watch him still on his knees.

"You must get the others," the fairies say to Elsabet, who, along with the whole undercity of vampires, is now walking forward. "Prepare all the village. We have extraordinarily little time."

CHAPTER 42

MOTHER

"What have you done?" Francis slams into Darius's office and grabs him. The wolves growl in person form. "Shut up, you mongrels." I have no patience. If I wasn't in a hurry, I would wipe them all out. I come through the door. I never have to travel anymore, so to deal with insolent behavior from these dogs when I have this problem will not do. Nina and Tarissa bow to the ground when they see me. That is lucky for them. Still, my anger makes me grab the first wolf and rip his head off.

"Get everyone ready. We are going to clean out all creatures on that little island forever." I talk directly to Melissa. The only one with a brain.

"Mother," Darius starts, but I leave without a word. He returned months ago and hoped no information would be found out.

"You should have told us. We would have kept her

here. She could have given us the fairy," Francis says as he leaves. Darius explains about Julie, the baby, and fairies.

"I have no choice, Darius," Melissa says.

"It has been four months. Why now?" Nina questions.

"Who knows?" Tarissa answers.

"Darius, I have to get ready now. Are you going to be beside me?" Melissa asks. This is the moment that she has been waiting for. She isn't going to let this opportunity pass, with or without him. A smile spreads across her face as she picks up her phone.

CHAPTER 43

SUSAN

Darius runs as fast as he can. He cries out in front of him. A warning cry. It is a cry he hasn't used for over 150 years. It was developed just between him and one other. Tears, blood-filled tears move from his eyes, past his ears, and find a resting place in his hair. Fear once again fills him. There is a vampire who he needs now. It has been so long, but only she can deal with the wave of carnage that is coming. His true equal. His family. He cries out his cry. The cry they had just for the two of them. He cries out to Elsabet with all his power and might, his feet still thundering toward the enemy of the last hundred years. They are his only hope to save Julie.

Elsabet and I are quietly watching our tribe practice. The new children are coming along nicely. They are so different from when they were in school in that town. They fight as well as any. Grant has balanced his whisper and shadow and is quite the leader, almost equal to Ryo.

Ten months, almost a year, and the village is wonderful. Alfred and Bonny are the mother and father of this village. Each person has added so much.

So many mated couples. The dream is starting again. Shinan-Hua and Darton, Kate and Bancroft, Raeleen and Young Sun, Lyesha and Jorn, and Anissa and Kyong all married.

Hope can start to come back to this family. Elsabet almost smiles. She looks at me and readjusts her face so I can't see how pleased she is. The night is just starting. The moon shows on one side of the sky as the sun sets on the other. It's just a sound, distantly familiar, comes to Elsabet and me. Everyone freezes. Elsabet knows the sound. She shakes her head as she tries to remember. As it comes again, it registers with Elsabet, and she's on it. I'm on it. It takes me more time to remember, but when I see her face, it comes back to me. Darius's warning cry.

"Now," she screeches. The other older vampires remember the cry at the same time and move quickly. "They are all coming to attack now," Elsabet screams as she moves fast through the village. "Get ready!"

I ready the warriors, vampire and human. The old and young humans and wolves make their way down to the underground city as wolves and vampires who have been sleeping come up armed and ready.

Darius comes through and falls at Elsabet's feet. The humans draw their weapons, the wolves are growling low and pacing, and the vampires are still but ready.

"Darius!" Julie breaks through the crowd and wraps her arms around him. This stupid girl.

"Elsabet, get her to safety. They are all on their way here." Darius carefully pushes Julie away from him. "An hour, maybe sooner, they are here." Elsabet puts her hand up, the villagers put away their weapons, and the wolves stop growling.

"Start from the beginning and be quick," Elsabet says. Behind her a fairy walks out. She passes Elsabet and stands in front of Darius. Darius lowers his head. A gasp rings out from all but the vampires. Alexandra, Mystic, Perival, Tybalt, and I gather closely around Elsabet.

"Are you here to protect what we love?" the little voice asks softly. She puts her hand on Darius's chin and lifts his head. Darius locks eyes with the fairy.

"Yes, I am."

"Welcome, father of fairy."

"We must hurry."

"Everything has its time." With that, the fairy turns and walks out.

"I take it you have met before?" Elsabet lifts her left eyebrow as she puts out her hand to Darius and helps him up. Julie moves to his side. I look at his first love and his new love. Glad to not be part of the group.

"They found out about Julie." Darius says as he puts his arms around Julie. "Mother and Frank are determined to wipe out all of you and Julie. We truly have little time. I know your humans can fight, but this is too big." He looks at Seth, Grant, Lance, Aaron, Penny,

Hannah, and Jasmine. "They don't know these humans are here. If they find them, it will be the end."

"You let me worry about them." Darius and I used to be close. He followed me like a puppy when he was first turned. A few hundred years later, we were like brother and sister. Never separated. He came to me when he had problems with Elsabet. Hell, even when he first had feelings for her, feeling different from most. We lost our attachment in a way, but he never did for her. His Elsabet. I don't think he has lost his feelings for her.

"They are ready. They have trained for this. What do you know about who can and who cannot?" Alexandra is holding back. She thinks they should start with Darius. Extinguishing him seems reasonable to most of the vampires. I understand how they feel, but still, he is Darius. I don't want to kill him. He actually could be the vampire who helps us move forward in this new overpopulated, picture-and-video-focused world. Tech is not a vampire's friend. Proof that the same person has been alive for hundreds of years doesn't bode well for our kind.

"Ha, miss your wit, Alex. Wish we had time to catch up, Babe." Darius flashes a smile.

CHAPTER 44

SUNG-GI

Ryo, Sung-Gi, Shinan-Hua, and Darton gather the human fighters together. Julie is sent to the underground city with some fairies and is unhappy. This is not the fairies' fight, nor is it Mystic's. The wolves are gathered within an earshot from the humans. The vampires are gone.

"What are we to do?" Kate is leaned up against Bancroft. "These kids aren't ready to fight."

"We do what we have been trained to do," Ryo says softly to Kate. "They can fight. They are ready, or they die. They must fight. They have trained well." He turns to the rest. "We know what to do! We start with the wolves." The wolves enclose the group at the invite. "You all stay in wolf form. You're stronger that way. Anissa and Lyesha, stay back with bow and arrow till you are out. Sung-Gi and Shinan-Hua, work as a team to start. It is what you know the best." Ryo catches my eye just for a moment.

"Raeleen and Vincent, use long swords. You two have a fresh style, but it is unbelievable. Kyong, Bancroft, Young Sun, Jorn, and Darton, you guys come along with me. I want knives on toes, knees, elbows. Do what you want for blade of choice. Kate, there is no one who can wield the swinging knives like you," Ryo continues. "The rest of you, hang back and keep ready with bow and arrow."

To the new arrivals, he gave this command: "Be ready to retrieve those who get hurt." Ryo directs the few others who can fight but don't have the training the other thirteen do. The young who have found refuge here ready themselves to care for those who get hurt. I watch the man I love explain the plan. He goes over the various stages of the fight. I feel like I am watching something that isn't part of me. I want to run to him and hug him. I don't want to fight. I want to save this little place. I am not scared. I am just sad about how their world is going to change. My husband doesn't look like he ever has. He seems so much bigger. As the vampires join us and we all work out the plan, I don't recognize any of them. Everyone seems so different.

"Sung-Gi?" Shinan-Hua whispers in my ear. "Are you crying?"

"Yes, but I don't know why." I shake my head and make a face at my sister.

"OK, everyone, get ready. Meet on the mountain edge. It's their only way in," Tybalt says. "You all know what to do. All of you come back alive, if you can." He pats Lance on the back.

"There is not much you don't know about fighting. We would not put you on the line if we did not think you could do this. You are ready. This is for the village. This is for your parents. This is for humanity, the human race. You are the future of humans," Perival says.

"Avenge your parents and all who died that day," Alexandra roars. Shouts go out across the village. She raises her spear and yells a warrior's yell.

CHAPTER 45

JASMINE

Half an hour later on the ridge of the mountain, a sea of wolves stand, and in the middle of them are young humans. Sung-Gi and Shinan-Hua have never looked so alike. Both have their hair back in three connecting ponytails. I have my hair in the same style. I stand slightly back from my sisters. I am terrified. I touch my high-collared metal choker. All of the humans have one. The twins' chokers were made with a right and left design. Sung-Gi wears the right, and Shinan-Hua wears the left. The only difference is the bangs that fall in Sung-Gi's face. On Shinan-Hua's left side stands Darton. On Sung-Gi's right side stands Ryo. This is now their village. They are the ones to protect it. The four feel the gravity of what they have been given. Behind them we stand, the newest of their clan. We all have neck collars, chest plates, upper-leg plates, and back plates. Most are embedded with retractable knives. It is heavy, but we have trained to hold the weight.

CHAPTER 46

THE ISLAND

On the shore below the gathering armed villagers, the vampires are lined up fifty yards from the beach. On the edge of the water, a group of vampires and small wolves gather, docking all kinds of watercrafts.

Darius stands at the top of a large rock to the left of the group.

"You cannot protect her, Son. I will forgive you if you just help us." Francis stands in front of an army of vampires and wolves.

"He will not help you this time, Father." Elsabet comes up beside Darius. The rest of the vampires line up. From the top of the mountain, the villagers and wolves crouch in readiness.

"Oh, my darling daughter." Francis smiles at his daughter in their vampire lives. "I have missed you." From above, the wolves start to run down the mountain. The first group of humans is riding on their wolves' backs. The young warriors have learned to stay on their wolves by placing one foot between the shoulder blades and the back foot on the widest part of the hip bone. Getting into a low squat was the key, but these young humans have practiced all their lives. It comes naturally to them.

As the opposing wolves come, Sung-Gi and Shinan-Hua start to run. Shinan-Hua jumps on Shik's back. She holds both her blades pointed toward her body, against the forearm. She gets her feet in place and lowers her body, then she reaches out her right arm without looking. Sung-Gi spins as she jumps and grabs her sister's hand with her right hand. Shinan-Hua uses all her strength and swings her sister across her and Shik as high as she can. The sisters let go, and Sung-Gi twists herself so she is facing the same direction as Shinan-Hua. She is suspended in air for a second. Shino leaps off another wolf to get greater air and comes up under Sung-Gi's waiting body. Riding their wolves side by side, the sisters get low and extract the blades they are carrying. Each hand holds its own blade. The sisters get even lower. Each kneels their back-left leg on the back of their wolf, holding their arms straight behind them, blades out like an extension of the arm. As a vampire jumps at Sung-Gi, she leans back, putting all her weight on her bent leg. Her head touches the heal of the foot on her bent leg. She brings her blades straight down along the side of Shino. She brings the blades up by her legs, crosses her arms, and reaches up, uncrossing them and bringing the knives in the neck of the vampire. At the same moment, Shinan-Hua jumps to her sister and comes across the side of the neck of the vampire, kneeing the body so it falls to the side. Shinan-Hua lands on the ground. Sung-Gi jumps off Shino and lands back-to-back with her sister.

Jasmine watches with both pride and fear. She readies her bow and arrow. She has gotten quite good in the last six months. Her job is to watch over her sisters with her bow. The same goes for Penny and Hannah. Each is to watch over their older siblings and shoot only when they are in trouble and there is a clear shot. Their wolves move on to battle more of the oncoming wolves. The sisters stand strong, back-to-back, ear to ear, arm to arm, with blades out. Two bodies working as one.

Raeleen and Kate are in another area fighting a group of vampires as more encircle them. Shinan-Hua and Sung-Gi run to them, blades out, pumping their arms with knife extensions as hard as they can. The sisters give new courage and strength to Kate and Raeleen. Raeleen twirls her twin blades, much longer than the twins' blades, back and forth, side to side, moving unpredictably toward one of the vampires. Raeleen spins her body around, blades out, and catches the vampire. A look of surprise is on the vampire's face as it hits the ground. The beautiful grace Raeleen puts in her style of fighting makes it look like a dance. It is stunning to watch. Penny copies some steps as she watches, before sending an arrow straight into the side of a wolf coming up behind Raeleen. Hannah and Jasmine aim their arrows and shoot again and again at the same wolf until he is down.

Kate takes on the opponent with a flurry of up-and-down slashing motions. Her small blades are connected by a chain. But she is keeping the blades close to her, swinging and slashing close to her head and body. A regular person would hold their breath waiting for her to hurt herself. Kate's fighting style is amazing, mostly because of her quiet nature. It has improved in the last couple of months with Hannah and Bancroft beside her. The vampire is hacked to pieces in a matter of seconds, and Kate moves on. The four girls regroup and ready themselves. Jasmine, Hannah, and Penny shoot arrows straight and hit the mark. The girls realize they need to pick off the same creature. The force is different from Anissa and Lyesha, who have been shooting all their lives.

Sung-Gi and Shinan-Hua are cut off from reaching Kate and Raeleen. They quickly position themselves and battle with all their might. The newly turned vampires are no match for them.

Anissa and Lyesha are pulling arrows hard and fast. Lyesha sees her wolf, Key, cornered by wolves. She runs forward and rips an arrow from the throat of a choking vampire. She pierces the skull of one of the wolves. Key fights two, ripping the necks open. Lyesha steps back to her original position beside Anissa. Both girls are feeling the pain in their shoulder and chest, but neither are slowing. Lyesha suddenly feels something on her head. It doesn't hurt; in fact, it is giving her a euphoric energy. She looks at Anissa, who is looking at her with a strange creature on her head. The creature is the size of a hand. It has a human face, but the nose is much larger and flops around. It has a white cap with a red ball on top. Its feet are like that of a tree frog. It had a bow-and-arrow set strapped to it. As strange as this little being is, Lyesha feels like she has seen it before. Small eyes and a forehead appear. The little creature on her head is bending over, talking to Lyesha. She can't understand the high-pitched sound but knows what they are doing. Her whisper communicates. She turns with the new energy and pulls her next arrow out. The feet on her head get tighter. A small arrow flies out before hers. It hit a wolf and disintegrates part of the flesh it hits. The girls pull arrow after arrow. They are accompanied by many of these creatures, although they only see the two. Little silver and gold arrows are everywhere. The creature's arrows don't kill, just dissolve parts of the opponent.

The fighting continues. The twins are in the middle. Sung-Gi runs up Shinan-Hua's back and stands on her shoulders. Sung-Gi jumps as Shinan-Hua lunges forward and slices the vampire standing in front of her. Sung-Gi steps one foot on the vampire's head and spins as she lands, stabbing the vampire through the neck from the back. They set up and get ready. Elsabet and Darius are doing the exact same moves, except they are using their hands instead of blades. The twin girls realize they have been taught the style that they heard stories about. The four move together. Vampires and humans. Moving and killing the same way.

Alexandra fights alone. Her long staff now holds arrow tips on each end. With precise and swift movements, she decapitates both wolves and vampires. She leaves a trail of bodies, and she moves through the crowd. Tybalt and a group of fifty or so vampires battle their way toward Francis and Mother. Perival and another group work with the human boys, fighting and protecting.

Darton, Ryo, Bancroft, Young Sun, Lance, Seth, Aaron, and Grant are fighting together. Bancroft is keeping an eye out for Kate. He knows how good she is. She doesn't know, so he glances over. There is not much he can do. The survival of the village is more important, so he cannot defend her, but he feels better checking. He knows this is against what she was taught. He can't help it. He loves her so.

Julie runs, having broken free from her house. She is trained to fight, and the strength from the fairy growing inside her gives her so much energy. Julie comes from the side closest to Francis. Renton springs into action a second before the rest. He is stopped by several city wolves. His pack is with him. Raeleen and Kate are about five feet from Julie when Kate hears Renton yelp. She stops and looks just as his hind leg is ripped open. Kate is frozen for a second. She turns just in time to see a wolf in midair coming for her. The wolf cries out and falls dead. Kate turns to see Raeleen get knocked on her stomach from behind. A wolf is on top of her and is ripping her back with his paws. Kate throws her knives out in front of her to cut the wolf down and runs top speed. The blood attracts and drives more of the younger vampires crazy. This makes them easier to kill. Kate stands straddling Raeleen. Julie runs to her. Jasmine, Penny, and Hannah send arrows flying. Penny starts to run forward. Jasmine and Hannah hold her down, dropping their arrows. The three girls watch the scene unfold. Kate and Julie fight over Raeleen's torn body. Julie saw Raeleen throw her sword and kill the wolf that was coming at Kate. She puts Renton out of her mind. She saw the rest of his pack surround him, so she knows he's alive. Julie fights hard, but Kate is stronger and faster. Julie misses her mark, and a vampire strikes her. Kate takes Raeleen's sword from the back of the dead wolf and slices clean through the vampire's neck. Julie is hurt, but she covers Raeleen with her body. Kate falters as Julie falls. "She can do it," the others are calling to Kate. She knows Bancroft is trying to get to her. She can't focus. She drops the large sword and is throwing her knives, but her arms are on fire.

"I love you, Kate! You can do this." Kate hears Bancroft in a slow, calm voice. "Empty your mind and breathe. You have got this. I will be there soon." Bancroft's words hit home for Kate. She looks at Raeleen and Julie on the ground.

"You just hang tight, Rae. I got you." Kate takes a deep breath and stills her mind. On her next breath in, she swings her leg behind her as a counterweight and throws both arms forward. The blades hit their target. She jerks the blades back to her body. The adrenaline pushes the muscle fatigue out of her mind. She breathes in again and explodes her arms out to the side. Again, the blades meet the mark. Kate fights on, dancing around Raeleen and Julie and throwing her blades with all her might. She's using her body to help shoot her blades and retract them back to her. Tears flow, although she doesn't notice. Penny, Jasmine, and Hannah gather themselves and resume shooting arrows. They work hard to protect Kate. The distance is far, and the girls' bodies are on fire, but they do not slow down. They work one wolf at a time.

Melissa runs to Renton. The village wolves crouch down, getting ready to attack. Wolves follow her, ready to kill. She spins when she gets to him and slices through the wolves that followed her. Melissa changed sides. Renton whimpers. "Save her, please."

At the same moment, Kate throws her blades out, and two vampires grab them. Kate unchains herself and grabs Raeleen's heavy blade again. She stands on top of Julie and Raeleen. With one blade she fights with everything she has. She is aware someone is fighting with her. She can't see or sense who it is. Her body starts to give out. She screams, cries, drops her blade, and covers the two beneath her. Waiting to feel the first strike, she thinks about how much she loves her village, her Bancroft, her beautiful sister, and her life. She is surprised she has not been killed yet. She looks up to see a vampire who looks like Julie, a blond-haired vampire and a dark-haired vampire, fighting to protect them. She was shocked but knew who they were at once. Darius, Elsabet, and Tybalt fight and carry out Julie, Raeleen, and Renton. Mystic leads Melissa, Nina, and Tarissa away with her. The rest of the village vampires leave the confused battlefield.

All the rest of Elsabet's vampires pull back. The other side pulls back, and seeing the vampires leave makes the opposite side slightly confused. Sung-Gi and Ryo stand together on the rock that Darius stood on in the beginning of this battle. The wolves and the rest have lined up. Silver and gold arrows are being used only when one of the opposing group steps forward. Francis and the other vampires smile when they realize there are no vampires around.

A sound that sends a chill through the whole island starts low. Every creature stops, unable to move. Both sides are still. Sakiya and Shino look at the humans and lower their heads. All the wolves from Elsabet's tribe back away and into the woods. Ten creatures shine in the moonlight with more behind. Bancroft takes Kate's hand. Kate can't figure out what is happening, but she is glad Bancroft is there. She doesn't know what these creatures are.

"Our fairies," Bancroft whispers as if reading her mind. She can't believe these are her little girls that pick flowers. She is scared of these things. Bancroft squeezes Kate's hand and signals with an upward nod for her to look forward, not at them. As the cries get closer, the human warriors get ready. Blades are out, and eyes are on the vampires and werewolves from the other side. Grant, Seth, Lance, and Aaron have been fighting and are bloody, but the adrenaline is flowing.

"Stop!" The mother of all vampires lifts Jasmine in the air. "You are also my children. You cannot kill *me*!" Her voice is so hard and cold. The fairies stop. When was Jasmine taken? The fairies stand, gnashing their jaws. The woman brings Jasmine to her lips and sinks her teeth into her. She then rips open her own wrist and pours her blood into Jasmine's mouth. She drops her body like a dirty rag on the ground and walks back to the waiting boat. The rest of her army follows.

"Mother! How dare you break your promise." Mystic's voice fills the air, but she is nowhere in sight. Mother's eyes widen in fear. Then she regains her composure.

The crowd rushes to Jasmine's body. Tiffy flies down, wailing large sounds of deep sorrow. The fairies lift Jasmine just as the rest get to her. "Please help her," Hannah sobs.

"Don't worry, child." The fairies seem incredibly old for the first time ever. Each fairy bit the tip of their finger and, in turn, placed a drop of blood on Jasmine's tongue. Mystic comes forward and says a prayer over Jasmine. The prayer is in a language no one understands. From the sky a white, glowing light comes down. It surrounds Mystic and Jasmine. All the fairies bow down low. They chant the strange prayer.

A glow comes from every pore of Jasmine's body. Jasmine's body rises on its own. The glow gets more intense. She shines. She gets so bright that everyone squints. The wolves edge out from the woods. Jasmine gets brighter and brighter as her body floats higher. Heat is radiating from Jasmine. All at once, her body explodes into flames. The group cries out in shock and sorrow. Out of the explosion, a huge bird on fire rises straight up. It cries and rushes the retreating vampires. The bird burns them and the boats that are remaining with a breath of fire. It flies over the fighters on the field and the fairies, then flies straight up again, and there's another explosion. A single feather floats to the ground. The second it hits the ground, it transforms into a naked Jasmine. She gives a light cough. The fairies and Mystic kiss her and leave.

When the vampires return, they find the group—humans, wolves, and all the creatures of nature—around Jasmine. Julie and Raeleen are with them.

"Jasmine is a phoenix. She can heal." Penny has figured it out as it was happening. She knew instinctively to bring the injured to Jasmine.

There have only been a few phoenixes in the whole history of the world. Our Jasmine is the last.

Made in the USA
Middletown, DE
25 April 2024